GUCCI GIRLS

by

TyeMease

CHAPTER 1

P-HALL WOKE UP OUT OF A DEEP SLEEP. NAYSIA LAID ON HIM with her arm still around his neck. They both were naked, only a blanket covered half of Naysia's butt. She was knocked out cold. P-Hall unwrapped her arm from around his neck, and then slid out of bed. Naysia smacked her lips, rolling over to another comfortable position, but never awoke. P-Hall put his clothes on, grabbed his phone, and keys then left.

A few hours later Naysia woke up to an empty sack. She wasn't really sweating it, she was used to P-hall leaving in the middle of the night. She got out of bed stretching her brown legs while reaching for the sky. She walked into the bathroom yawning. After a fifteen-minute shower she came back out of the bathroom with a big towel wrapped from her breast down. She had another that she was drying her hair off with. She looked at her phone and seen that she had two missed calls. After checking the numbers she hastened to get dressed. She grabbed her Birkin bag and headed out to make her rounds.

****

Naysia's heels clicked against the floor as she approached her friend from behind. He sat inside of the starbucks typing away on his laptop.

"Sorry to keep you waiting Web," Naysia said.

She ran her hand from one side of his shoulder to the other. He looked up happy to see her. He stood up, hugged, and kissed her on the cheek.

"Its alright, I'm more patient than most". They both sat down, he closed his laptop, and focused on her. "I took the liberty of ordering you some coffee," Web said sliding the Starbucks bag and cup of coffee to her side of the table.

"How thoughtful," Naysia said smiling.

It would always seem to be some sexual tension between the two when they were alone, but either of them ever went any farther than being too friendly, which was actually their way of flirting. The subject of them hooking up was taboo for many reasons. The only reason they ever met up was to handle business.

Halfway through her coffee Naysia dug into her Birkin bag pulling out another bag handing it to him under the table. The sly move went unseen by any of the others around them. Already knowing the contents of the Starbucks bag she received from him she put it in her purse.

"Thanks for the coffee, Next time it's on me," Naysia said getting up from her seat. She fixed her dress, picked up her bag and hooked it around her shoulder.

"Now what kind of gentlemen would I be if I let you pay for our date?" Web had a big smile on his face looking up at her.

"You'll be the kind of gentlemen that thinks he's on a date when he's not." Naysia smiled back shaking her head as in disbelief. "You'll be alright," She said walking by tapping him on the shoulder.

****

"You like this shirt," Stacy asked holding up a Gucci shirt?

"Let me see. You can't fit this, let me have it," Trudy said.

Stacy took her shirt out of Trudy's hands. "Watch me squeeze right into it. Everything I got super tight."

"Wait until ya'll see this Gucci dress I picked up," Jinger said.

"You talking about that cream one," Trudy asked?

"Yup."

"I seen it. It is nice."

"I'ma wear it tonight. Aint none of them bitches going to be able to fuck with me in there," Jinger said as she got up and began sashaying towards the exit. Her friends followed as their train came to a halt at the Camden Transportation center.

****

Jinger had finish putting her make up on. It was a little past nine O'clock, she had been waiting for her ride. Earlier after they came from shopping, she had gone to sleep exhausted from all them hours spent on her feet. She planned on it being a long night, and she definitely planned on turning up. Her little brother had came in the room, she turned towards him and asked, "How do I look?"

"Like a prostitute," he responded not giving her too much of a look.

"Shut up, you just mad because you gay."

"Whatever, your friends are here for you," he said before walking back out of the room. He had an attitude like he wasn't beat for his older sister.

Shay, Trudy, and Stacy were waiting in the car for Jinger.

"What took you so long," Jinger asked once she got in the car?

"All that matter is that we're here now." Trudy responded while pulling off.

"I can't believe ya'll went over Philly without me," Shay complained.

"You were nowhere to be found," Jinger replied.

"Is that where you got that dress?"

"This and some other stuff. Everything I stole is official," Jinger said boasting.

Jinger and her friends were boosters, they did whatever they had to do to have the best things. Growing up in Centerville projects on welfare they never had much, so stealing was their go to move. For them it was only two types of gals, go getters, and go diggers. They strived for the former, yet all they tried to mess with was dudes who they thought had money, and street fame. The difference between them and gold diggers was they didn't just give up the ass and expect handouts. They weren't satisfied with anybody baby feeding them, they went and got theirs regardless.

****

The bouncer at the door was hesitant about letting Jinger in because she looked so young. He tried to make all of them show I.D... Instead of showing I.D. Trudy called the promoter and handed the bouncer the phone. That move got all of them in free.

"Who you know," Jinger asked Trudy?

"This Tye event. You might know him, He a little older than me."

When they got in there Jinger began looking around. Everyone was looking fabulous. It was a no hoodie, sneakers, or white-T type of event. That kept a lot of broke bum dudes away. Instead of it having a club atmosphere, it was more of a social event, with good laid-back music playing.

"Look at these fake as Housewives of Atlanta chicks. Aint that little red head hoe too young to be in here. I should get her kicked out," Jacinica vehemently said.

Qadir who was standing near by turned around trying to see who Jacinica was going on like that. Once he seen that it was Shay and Trudy he made his way over to them. Shay lit up when she saw her cousin. They gave each other a big hug.

"Ya'll looking good. I'ma have to protect ya'll from these predators in here," Qadir said.

"Best believe we aint the prey," Shay bantered.

"Sure not, this the bait right here," Trudy said smiling with her right hand on her hip and her ass poked out to the side.

Qadir smirked at Trudy in her freak em dress. "What's the name of that dress?"

"Gucci," Trudy replied like what else could it had been."

"Is it real," he asked joking?

"Of course, we aint none of these bootleg hoes running around out here," Stacy chimed in.

"Ma bad ma bad, I didn't mean to offend none of The Gucci Girl's. I was just messing with ya'll. You got some feisty friends cousin. Maybe I shouldn't tell ya'll that ya'll friend got a hater," Qadir said looking at Jinger.

"Who hating on my girl Jinger," Shay asked?

"Jacinica."

Jinger was looking a little shocked until she heard the name. "I'm not worried about her. Her old ass just mad because her man on ma dick." Jinger looked over where Jacinica was and rolled her eyes.

"I'ma be over here if you need me cousin," Qadir said before stepping off to go mingle with his peoples.

Jinger was looking a little agitated so Trudy put her arm around her and they began walking.

"Don't worry about her, we didn't come here for any of that. Trust me she don't want to get that cheap as wig snatched off," Trudy said trying to bring her friend back to a cheerful state.

It worked, Jinger began laughing, and tried to sideline the negative thoughts. They mingled, mainly with dudes. The night was going well, everyone was enjoying themselves. Still what Qadir had told them was on her mind. She tried to make sure she knew where Jacinica was at all times. They caught eye contact a few times. As the night went on Jinger had tried to let go of the situation. Her and her girls were flirting with the fellas, drinking bottles. The promoter Tye walked over to them. He shook the dudes hands who they was talking to, and they had a few words. It was clear that they knew him.

"What's up ladies," Tye said walking over to Trudy.

Her friends watched Trudy light up as he hugged her.

"He hitting that, that's how we got in free," Shay whispered to Jinger causing her to giggle.

"What are ya'll giggling about," Stacy asked?

"Damn nosy, you can't be in on everything," Shay told her laughing.

They were all feeling nice from the liquor. The dudes they were at the table with were cool, but Jinger wasn't feeling any of them. She wasn't even trying to take one for the team. Shay kept reminding her that they had money, but she didn't care. It was three dudes. Shay and Stacy had their dudes they were talking to. Trudy was good, she was talking to Tye. Since it was getting late it looked like she was going to be leaving with him, Jinger gave the other dude some conversation, but she really wasn't feeling him. He was too ugly, short, and skinny. Out of all the dudes he was with he looked like the broke one. She remained friendly, especially since everything was on him and his boys.

"Ya'll ready to leave," Trudy asked walking back over to them?

"We good," Stacy said. "We got our ride."

"I'm ready," Jinger said getting up out of her seat. "Drop me off."

"You leaving me," Cody asked?

"Yeah, I have to get home."

"Here, let me give you my number," he insisted.

As soon as Jinger got up all the wine she had drank hit her. She stumbled to the side a little bumping into somebody, spilling the drink she was holding on her new cream dress. She turned around looking to blame her clumsiness on whoever bumped her. When she looked up she saw Jacinica. Cody quickly saw the pretty soft-spoken beauty he was chatting up become belligerent.

"Bitch watch where the fuck you going," she blurted out.

"Bitch, you the…."

"Bang!" Jinger hit her in the face with the glass she was holding. They threw a couple punches, but the fight was quickly broken up. Cody pulled Jinger back and was holding her.

"You fat bitch," Jinger yelled trying to break Cody's grip. He held her tight not letting her go.

Jacinica yelled back obscenities as she was being pulled away by her friends. Shay came out of nowhere swinging a hard over hand punch striking Jacinica across the face. "Bitch," she yelled. Jacinica grabbed her face, she started crying going crazy. Tye grabbed Shay holding her so she couldn't do anything else. Qadir seen him grab her and ran over there.

"What you doing to my fam," he asked taking her out of his grasp.

Before Tye could say anything Trudy stepped in. "He was breaking it up Qadir." Trudy was embarrassed, she quickly got her girls out of there.

Jinger was in the backseat ranting talking about what she was going to do to Jacinica.

"You won Jinger. Now shut up, you're drunk," Trudy said driving tired of hearing her.

She looked over at Stacy, Stacy started shaking her head. The whole situation blew all of their mood. They had intentions on leaving with the fellas they were chilling with. They didn't get all sexy so their night could end wack. By the time they got back to Camden Jinger was knocked out sleep. They tried to wake her up, to no avail, so they carried her in the house.

CHAPTER 2

JINGER WOKE UP TO THE CONSTANT RINGING OF THE DOORBELL. "Hold up, Shit," she said stumbling all the way to get the door. Her eyes peered through the sun rays as she held the door open trying to focus on who was ringing like they were crazy. Her aunt stood there looking at her.

"You look horrible, I like that dress though," Naysia said entering the house. Jinger followed behind her. She was actually happy to see her aunt. She was just too hung over to show it.

"These cute, they yours," Naysia asked checking out Jinger's shoes?

She wouldn't wear them because she had money, but all the chicks who couldn't afford red bottoms were wearing them. Jinger nodded her head yeah.

"You went out last night? Who let a seventeen-year-old party in their club? I'ma get to the bottom of this," Naysia joked.

"I'm not seventeen, I'm eighteen," Jinger blurted then plopped on the couch to lay back down.

"You got fucked up last night, I can tell. You got red wine all on ya dress. Look at you," Naysia said smiling looking at her thinking how much she had grown.

Jinger looked down at her dress in disappointment. She sucked her teeth then said," this was brand new."

"The cleaners will get it out. I got some old dresses and shoes you might like too. A few of them still got the tags on them."

"When are you going to bring them," Jinger asked excited about the thought. She knew all her aunt wore was the fliest stuff.

"I'll bring them soon. Where ya mom at?"

"I don't know where she went. I had just woken up when you came."

Naysia pulled a seat up at the dining room table. She sat her Birkin bag on her lap, dug in it and pulled out a Dutch. "You smoking," she asked digging in her pocket pulling out a fifty or sour? Naysia asked a rhetorical question, she knew everything that her niece was into. She was once her age, and at her age it wasn't much she wasn't into.

Jinger looked at her aunt. They didn't have a tight relationship like Jinger would have liked. She didn't even know exactly what her aunt did for a living, or how she stayed so fly. All she knew was that she was live, and that she wanted to be like her.

"This your last year of school right," Naysia asked passing Jinger the dutch?

"Yeah, we graduate in a couple of months."

"What are you going to do then? Don't be like me. I was always smart, but when I graduated I was like ok, now what. I went to college for a semester, then I was fed up with school. A job was out of the question. That shit'll fuck up ma fly. I can't have that," she said laughing.

Jinger started laughing too, choking off of the smoke. Naysia began patting her on her back.

"Whatever you decide make sure it pays well, because the cost of living is high. You'll see when you get on your own. You like nice things too. You better get a dude with some money.

When Jinger's mom and brother came back they were at the table with a bunch of junk food munching away. Naysia smiled at her sister with low eyes while Jinger ate the crunchy cheese doodles like they were the best tasting snacks ever.

****

"Why ya'll do that to my brother's girlfriend," Laquanda asked laughing.

Trudy was sitting on her step in her shorts, flip flops, and a head scarf. She began shaking her head at the question, clearly still upset.

"Aint nobody do nothing to that girl. She started it running her mouth. Jinger gave her what she was asking for."

"Ma mom said that she got a nice dounut."

"I think Shay did that. She couldn't even see no more after Shay hit her, she just started screaming. They messed up my night though. I was trying to leave with Tye. Now I gotta call him to see what's up. Which reminds me," Trudy said going into the house to get her cellphone so she could make that call.

"Hope we didn't ruin your night," she said once Tye answered the phone.

"Not at all, that was a cat fight. As long as it wasn't any dudes trying to kill each other I'm good. It was basically the let out anyway."

"I still feel bad about the situation."

"Well we can get together tonight and work on making you feel better," Tye suggested.

"That sound good to me, what time are you talking," Trudy asked?

"I'll be there at eight."

****

Trudy cleaned up nice as if she was going on an official date. At least that's what she told everyone else. Tye took her straight to his house in Haddonfield.

"You live here by yaself" she asked looking around?

"Yeah, Why?"

"Nothing, it's just a nice house."

Trudy was impressed at the four bedrooms, two bathrooms, two car garage, two thousand square foot home. She didn't personally know anybody that had a house like it. She looked at all of the security cameras he had in each room and wondered if he was legit like she thought then why would he need them. The thought of it made him more interesting to her.

"You ready to make that up to me," Tye asked?

"Make it up to you? You make it seem like I owe you something."

"Nah, you don't owe me, from the way you was talking I kind of figure you had something for me."

"I got something for you. It depends what you're talking about," Trudy said blushing.

"You know what I'm talking about." He bear hugged her and kissed her on the cheek." I see you like playing games, huh?

"Is that a pool," Trudy asked? She saw the pool through the window.

"Yeah, you trying to go chill in it? I keep the water temperature nice and warm," He told her that so she wouldn't be afraid to get in. "Come on, we going out there. Let me go get us something to smoke and drink first."

Tye came out with a fifth of Hennessey, and some weed. Trudy was in the pool already hanging on the edge looking at him. She looked like she had taken a swim already. She definitely wasn't one of those chicks that didn't want to get their hair wet. She smiled as her jet-black hair draped down pass her shoulders. When he seen that she was naked a smirked flashed across his face.

"You just couldn't wait, huh? How's the water?

"It's a little chilly, but I won't be worried about that when you get in here."

He quickly put the henny and weed down, stripped ass naked then canon balled into the pool causing a big splash. Trudy turned around so the water wouldn't splash in her face. She grabbed the henny and poured them both a drink. As she turned back around he arose from the water right in front of her, both of his arms on the ledge trapping her between them. She smiled and gave him his glass. He took the glass and pressed his naked body against hers. She felt his swag on her. He drank a little from his glass then sat it on the ledge. He began kissing her, then lifted her legs up pinning her to the side of the pool. Him penetrating her made her felt so good she dropped her glass in the water. She wrapped her hands around the back of his head and their bodies made its own rhythm creating small waves in the water.

CHAPTER 3

It was lunch time at Camden High School. This was the times when almost no one went to class. Three lunch periods back to back had students in the cafeteria when it wasn't their lunch period. Jinger was heading to the back of the line to buy her food. For some reason she was to good for what they served on the trays. James stuck out his hand for her to get in front of him so she wouldn't have to go all the way to the back of the line.

"Thank you," Jinger said taking him up on his offer.

James always treated Jinger nice. He liked her, and she knew it. Even though he was a handsome guy he wasn't her type. He was a good dude. He went to every class and did all his schoolwork. In the hood that's considered a minus instead of a plus. He didn't even have a nick name, that's how cool he wasn't.

"You're welcome Jinger. I been wanting to ask you something." He stood there looking at the side of her bright burgundy died hair. "Would you like to go to the prom with me?"

"You should have said something before. I would have gone with you. I'm already going with somebody now," she told him as if he had a legitimate shot.

"I figured that. Aye, it didn't hurt to ask." James didn't really feel let down. He knew it was a long shot that she'll say yes, but he felt that it was worth a try.

There was an awkward silence until Jinger got her food and left. She felt bad letting him down, but the truth was even if she didn't have a date she still wouldn't have went with him. The prom was just for show, it was the corny part. It was after the prom that Jinger was really looking forward to.

School is going to be over next month, and Jinger couldn't wait, she was going to be relieved. It was an inconvenience for her. She felt like nothing they taught was going to be applicable to her daily life.

Eventually Naysia Brung Jinger them clothes and shoes that she said she was going to bring her. Jinger was feeling like she had just went shopping. Even the ones Naysia had wore were still in good condition. A few of them were brand new. She tried all of them on, doing so she found one that looked so good on her that she wanted to wear it to the prom. She took a picture of the dress and sent it to her date because he was supposed to be getting his clothes soon. His colors were going to match hers. She had everything set up. Her date wanted to rent a limo for the occasion. She told him not to bother, that she had the wheels. He was kind of curious about what she had in mind, because he knew that she didn't have a car, but he went along with it.

****

P-Hall had some free time on his hands from making his rounds so he rode through Waterloo Street, one of his dope blocks. He noticed things wasn't how they should be. It was dudes out there hugging the blocks, but it seemed like not enough fiends was showing them any love. He was wondering where they were at. His mans Bop was on the steps talking to some chicks. He cut the conversation short when he saw P-Hall's white corvette pull up.

"What's going on out here," P-Hall asked as soon as Bop got in the car.

Bop shrugged his shoulders. "Ezel renting the block to some dudes. They got some shit out there called Rob Ford. (Names after that Canadian Mayor that had become famous for partying and doing drugs) It's shutting everything down.

"You got a lot left"?

"I still got most of it."

"What!"

"Bout time we get to the rest of that shit its going to be like a three. I'm telling you nothing been coming through."

P-Hall was absorbed in thought, he didn't like that. The block had a quota to meet and if it didn't meet its quota then he wouldn't be able to meet his quota. Which meant that the churches chicken was being messed up.

"Yo, you gotta handle that," he said looking at Bop seriously.

"You mean handle it handle it?"

"Yeah."

"All right. No problem," Bop said and exited the vehicle.

P-Hall knew the only way to get the traffic back around there was to make their block hot so they wouldn't be able to do anything for a couple of days, and at the same time maybe the dudes Ezel was renting the block to would leave.

****

The next day around six in the morning fiends were lined up on the set camping out like they were waiting outside of a best buy on black Friday. A black Lincoln with dark tints pulled up and let two dudes out then pulled off. The fiends were happy as Catholics seeing the pope. One of them even yelled amen. The line led to the alleyway, that's where the two dudes headed with the two big bags full of dope. Once they began serving the fiends the line started moving. While they were serving two fiends skipped everybody else going straight to the front of the line. All the other fiends were complaining, but the dudes didn't pay them any mind.

"Get the fuck in line like everybody else," one of the trappers told the one with the grey hood over his head.

Dudes trapping wasn't really paying attention to who they was serving. It was too much traffic. They was just trying to get some order so they could get them out of there. They were giving out drugs and stuffing money in their pockets. Neither of them seen it coming, they just heard a fiend yell, "They got guns!" That's when the shots rang out, about twenty of them. Afterwards the two dudes who was thought to be fiends ran around the block to a car that was waiting for them. The other two dudes were laying on the ground fighting for their lives. Dope bags had fallen, Fiends were shoving each other, tussling, even falling on the two dying dudes trying to pick up as many bags as they could.

CHAPTER 4

"Where ya car at," Jiger asked not seeing Scoob's pearly white S 550 Benz sitting out front?

That's what he was driving the first day he had swept her off her feet. She had just finished getting her hair done and she was feeling herself. She had a little extra sway in her hips as she walked down the street. He saw how them tight jeans was hugging her and pulled up a long side of her, slow riding while trying to hollah at her through the passenger side window. Before seeing him she saw the car. It didn't matter who it was as long as he wasn't broke. She was flattered. He pulled the car over and she gave him some play. They got freaky a few times after that day and she peeled him for a couple of dollars a few times, but it was always for something light. Fifty to a hundred here and there.

"Ma mom got it," Scoob responded to her question.

This was the first time Scoob had invited Jinger to his actual home. Usually they'll go to the motel. She scoured the place as she walked through. It was a nice house in Pennsauken. It was clear that he didn't live there alone. She thought it was too much of a home for a street dude, unless he was gay and from her experience with him he couldn't have been that.

"You got a girlfriend that live here with you, or something," she asked?

"Nah."

"Where are we going?"

"Down the basement," Scoob responded.

Down the basement, Jinger thought to herself. *Why the hell are we going down there?*

When they got down there it looked masculine, more like it was his place. It had the unmade bed, big bean bag, pizza box with left over pizza in it, and a T.V. With an Xbox hooked to it. Scoob began picking up things, trying to straighten up a little.

"You can sit down," Scoob said after clearing the bed for her. He took his coat off the bed and threw it in the chair full of clothes.

"I'll be right back," he said, and went up stairs.

Jinger looked around frowning as the reality dawned on her. She started to feel like a sucka, like she'd been tricked. She shook her head and exhaled in disappointment, but she was mad at herself more than anything. Jinger straighten her face out when he came back, he was smiling. She just sat there with her legs crossed.

"You alright," he asked? He sat next to her and kissed her on the neck.

She didn't want to say anything to him. Scoob jumped back on the bed.

"Come on, watch this movie with me,"

I don't want to watch no fucking movie, she thought to herself.

"Why we down this basement?"

"Because I don't feel like dealing with my parents."

She was younger than him, but she thought about how immature he sounded talking about his parents.

"I thought you had your own place."

"I do, I stay in Lindenwold, this is home base though."

Jinger wasn't in the mood to watch a movie, but she ended up watching it anyway. They laid on the bed hugged up. The whole time she was pissed, but she had a hidden agenda.

"You know I graduate in a couple of weeks, right?"

"Congratulations," Scoob said patting her on the butt. She forced a change in her mood and snuggled up against him. He kept watching the movie not thinking much about what she just told him.

"Can I take the Benz to the prom?"

"I can't let you use that."

"Why not?"

"Because it's not mine."

"Whose is it"?

"Its ma moms."

"I thought it was yours."

"I never told you that, that's what you assumed."

Jinger became livid. She couldn't believe her prom was about to be ruined because of this scrub. The whole time she thought that she had him in her palm to the point she would be able to use the Benz. She pushed herself off his chest and got up.

"You be lying, lose my number you fucking loser," she said before storming off.

Scoob looked shocked, wondering why she bugged out on him like that. They were just chilling enjoying a good movie he thought. When things didn't go Jinger's way she didn't care about the world, everybody could go to hell if she couldn't get what she wanted.

Jinger wanted to say forget the prom but a part of her really wanted to go. She didn't just want to show up in a limo like everybody else. She wanted to shine and outshine everybody else. She wanted to be driving something sweet so she could show people how she was doing it.

****

P-Hall let Bop in his condo and kept talking on his phone. Bop went to the table and started taking money out of the bag. The money was wrapped in thousand stacks. All dirty money, which meant a lot of ones, fives, tens, and twenties. Each stack looking more than what it actually was.

P-Hall pinned the phone between his ear and shoulder while using his hands to light the dutch.

"Alright, I'ma see you soon," he said. He took the phone off of his ear and ended his call then took a couple of pulls of the dutch while walking towards Bop.

"Shit back normal. That other shit taken care of too. I don't know if they knew we had anything to do with it or not."

"They got an Idea. I just got off the phone with Baby-K. He aint say much on the phone, I gotta get with him about the whole thing. I know that's what he was talking about because it just happened."

"What..., did it sound like he didn't approve?"

"It aint that, He know dude whose block it is. I'll find out what's going on. Just make sure everybody on point out there in case dudes try some bullshit."

Bop heard a noise coming from the bedroom, when he looked Naysia was coming out. She walked up to P-Hall kissed him on the cheek then said, "All the money is on the dresser. Hey Bop," She said and waved.

"What's up Naysia? She a true rider. I wish I had one of them," Bop said once she left.

"Yeah, she thorough," P-Hall said not thinking much of it.

****

"Hello," Naysia said answering her cellphone?

"Aunt Naysia, I need a favor. You know I don't ask for much, but ma prom coming up and the ride I had fell through. Now I don't have a car. Can I use yours?"

"What's wrong with your moms," she shot back jokingly.

"I can't look fly in that, it's too plain. Come on now Aunt Naysia, you know how it is on prom night."

"I know how it is. Usually the guy is supposed to supply the ride. I got you though, when is it?"

"On the 16th."

"Alright, I won't forget."

Naysia didn't mind letting her niece use her car, she knew her prom meant a lot to her. As she talked on the phone, she didn't even notice the police car behind her.

"I have to call you back," she told Jinger.

She ended the conversation, then tried her best to drive steady. It was too late the cop had put on his sirens. "I can't believe this," Naysia said to herself as she pulled over. She sat patiently waiting for the cop to get out of his car. She didn't have anything incriminating in the car so she wasn't worried. Her first thoughts were that the cop was hating on her car. He had to be hating, why else would he pull her over she thought. She was looking through the rearview mirror when she saw the tall dark handsome man in uniform exiting the cop car. Feeling like she had to tighten up a bit, she started checking her mirror, looking at her face making sure her makeup was good, and that there wasn't any crust or anything in her eyes. Before she knew it he had tapped on the window. She rolled it down trying to play it cool.

"Do you know why I pulled you over," the officer asked? He was so tall that he had to bend down to look in the car.

Dam he look good, I hope he not a dickhead, Naysia thought as he asked the question. "No, I do not officer, why?"

"You were driving while on your cellphone." He pulsed waiting for her to deny it like everyone else did but she didn't say anything. "You do know that's illegal, right," he asked taking his pen and ticket pad out?

"Yes, I do and I'm sorry. I was wrong."

The cop smiled at her. "Look, I tell you what, I'ma give you a verbal warning this time. Just be mindful when you're driving. You could kill someone, or even yourself. Nearly 70% of all accidents occur because people want to be on their cell phones texting or talking. So, try to be more mindful, alright? Smile a little too, you're too pretty to be looking so serious."

Naysia smirked, trying her hardest to hold back from smiling. "Thank you officer."

"I don't usually do this, especially when I'm on duty, but can I get your number so I can give you a call? Maybe we can go out, get to know each other a bit."

Without hesitation Naysia gave him her number so she could get out of there.

****

Baby-K rode up in a black Cadillac Escalade. P-Hall got out of his car and into the truck with him.

"What's going on out here," Baby-K asked P-Hall?

"Things was slow, them dudes on Hope had some good shit. It was shutting everything down so I sent a couple of dudes around there. I didn't figure they would think that it was going to come from us. I know we wasn't the only ones flow they were affecting."

"They don't really know. Everybody a suspect to them right now. Ezel tried to hit me with the bullshit though. He was talking like he knew that I had it done. I let him know he mistaken, that I didn't have anything to do with that. Rather he believed me or not, it don't matter. I never did trust him so stay on point," Baby-K told P-Hall.

"Always," P-Hall responded.

****

Baby-K don't like to show his face much. He tries to do his thing from afar at the same time stay in tune with everything involving his money. Him and Ezel was once the best of friends, selling dope on the same block. When Ezel decided he wanted his own him and a couple of dudes he had influence over opened a set a couple of blocks down. The extra competition caused bad blood between them and a beef broke out. They were actually trying to kill one another. There were a few shoot outs, but no one ever got killed. Because of this they were able to mutually agree to piece things up. Still they never trusted one another. That's why even though Baby-K told Ezel that his peoples didn't have anything to do with this last incident, he knew Ezel didn't believe him, and probably didn't trust him.

CHAPTER 5

Jinger and her prom date Brah were outside of her house taking pictures. Her mom and friends were out there also. The whole time she was waiting on her aunt for the car. About fifteen minutes after they began taking pictures Naysia pulled up in her white F-type Jaguar, freshly detailed. She got out looking just as or if not finer than her car.

"Stop looking at my aunt," Jinger told her prom date. He couldn't take his eyes off of her.

"You thought I wasn't going to come," Naysia said giving Jinger a hug.

"You took long enough. I was prepared to take my moms car."

"You don't want to show up in that thing, you'll really get clowned."

They both started laughing. The only person who knew why they were laughing was Brah.

"Make sure you take good care of my niece," Naysia told him.

"I got her," he responded.

"Come on, let me get in some of these pictures with ya'll," Naysia said wrapping her arms around them as they posed.

****

"Ya aunt looking right, I think she feeling me too. I had ma hand all on her butt while we were flicking it up. She aint say nothing, that's how I know she feeling me."

Jinger knew Brah was just messing with her. She turned her face up and kept driving. "You're not her type."

"You trying to say I don't look good enough for your aunt, because it don't get too much better than me," Brah said like he belonged on people's cover of top 100 sexiest men a live.

"Just because you easy on the eye don't mean you're her type."

"What's her type?"

"Dudes that get money and do big things. You do neither," she said giggling.

Brah was feeling some kind of way but what could he say, she was right. The way she said it made him feel like the money he was getting in the streets was nothing.

****

Jinger pulled up in style just like she wanted. She was getting all the attention. A couple dudes came in some big cars, but she was the only female who up in something sweet. Everybody else had regular cars and limos.

They had a little fun at the prom dancing, socializing, and carrying on. After the prom they went to a liquor store. Brah had a fiend he knew go get them a bottle of henny. Then they went to his house. As soon as they got in his room he cracked the bottle of henny took a big gulp then passed it to her.

"When are you going to get your own place? You selling all them drugs, you should have some money saved," Jinger said looking around at what seemed like a human pig pin. The room was having an effect on her mood. She didn't feel like it was an appropriate setting for the attire they were wearing. The whole thing started to remind her of the loser Scoob who she thought had money but was still living with his mom. The only difference was that she knew Brah wasn't big time. Plus, she had love for Brah but she was tired of dealing with losers. She felt that she deserved better.

"I'm good, I got everything I need and it's free. You can't beat that."

"So, ten years from now you still going to be living with your mom for free?"

"I don't know, I don't even know what I'ma be doing tomorrow you talking about ten years from now. Man, drink up," Brah said giving her back the bottle.

He lit a Black and Mild and looked at her crazy for asking the questions she was asking. Jinger just shook at her head at his stupidity.

"Why you asking all these questions? Come here so I can get that dress off of you."

While Jinger realized that she was dealing with an idiot that idiot always gave her good dick, and that's what she was trying to end her night off with. She took that dress off and they began getting it in.

****

"Can I get my car," Naysia asked over the phone?

"Oh, I'm sorry. Here I come now," Jinger said.

She had just woke up when she received a phone call. She rushed to put some clothes on then left.

"You enjoyed yourself," Naysia asked when Jinger walked through the door?

"It was alright," Jinger responded handing her the keys.

"I told that boy to have you home at a decent time. That meant he wasn't supposed to try to get any," Naysia joked.

"I didn't mean to fall asleep."

"Fall asleep wasn't the only thing you did. I'm not sweating that. Look, since you a big girl now I'ma come get you sometimes, take you somewhere we can have fun."

"I'm cool with that. Don't forget you told me that because I won't"

"I know you not."

****

Jinger prom was a PG version of when she goes out with her friends. The main plus was that she was the main attraction. From the car she pulled up in, to the dress she wore. She felt like she was the hottest chick there that night. Being the youngest in her crew she was usually the runt. All her friends looked good, that was a requirement to be around them. A chick needed to be a seven and a half at least. That was just in the face. The body is what a take them over the top.

Jinger is a long legged 5'8, fat butt, flat stomach, real light skin with bright burgundy hair. She dyed her hair that color and liked it so much that she never changed it back. It ran concurrent with her skin tone making her look exotic. The make up she always wore accentuated her features even more, causing her to look a little older. Exactly what she was going for. Where she was from not too many chicks her age wore make up. She been wearing it ever since she been hanging out with an older crowd.

****

"How was ya prom," Laquanda asked?

"It was alright, nothing serious," Jinger responded.

"Where did ya'll go afterwards?"

"To his place," Jinger said turning up her face.

"The one he lives in with his mommy," Laquanda said laughing.

"Yeah right, for some reason I keep ending up with duds. I asked him when is he going to move out." He said, "for what, that he got it good there." "I definitely have to fall back from him. He got a loser mentality."

Her friends were laughing at the way she said it and the faces she was making.

"Ma brother not a loser," Laquanda said in her brother's defense since he was one of the dudes Jinger be messing with.

"Yes he is, he just got more money than all the other ones I deal with. Plus he got a girl. He not really ma dude."

"You had dude from the outskirts with the Benz, what happened with him," Trudy asked?

"That was his mom car. They got money not him. He twenty-eight years old sleeping down his parent's basement playing video games."

"Shit they aint going to be around forever. You could fall back until some of that inheritance money come through," Laquanda joked.

"Why didn't you give Cody any play that night we were at the club? Told you he had it," Trudy said.

"You talking about the skinny, ugly dude? He wasn't my type."

"He got money that's every girl type."

"Well he didn't look like he had money that night."

"Them be the ones that be really having it. The ones that be looking like they got it be the ones fronting," Laquanda chimed in.

"All them dudes that was around him that was iced out spending all that money are apart of his squad. He the leader," Trudy said.

"What about Shay cousin, Dude Qadir? He was looking good that night," Jinger said seeming interested.

"Every time I hear something about him it's about him beefing, shooting, or killing somebody. He be laying low, but every time I see him he be looking like money. He must be doing something right," Trudy said.

What Jinger had just heard about Qadir would have kept many females away from him but Jinger wasn't an ordinary female. The fact that he was into all of that stuff and wasn't dead or in jail excited her. It told her that he was not only thorough but smart as well. All of which made her more interested in him. She thought about his sinister look. For her it only added to his sex appeal.

****

Steve pulled out the chair for Naysia. She sat down and he helped her scoot under the table.

"I hope this is not too fancy for you," Steve said being sarcastic.

"You funny, is pulling women over how you get all your dates?"

"Ok, you got me. I'm a little ashamed of that, I'm not going to lie. I'm a person that believes when you want something you should go after it, you never know if you'll get that opportunity again."

"So, you seen something you liked?"

"Someone," he said correcting her.

Naysia began blushing looking at the menu. So far she liked the corny feeling she was getting on her date with Steve. He brought a smile to her face and made her laugh. She wasn't used to messing with a dude who wasn't in the streets. Messing with a cop in particular was like blasphemy. It literally went against her sacred beliefs. At first she had only accepted to go on the date to get out of a ticket, but while on the date she had a good time with him and could see herself going out with him again.

"Thank you for the dinner," Naysia said as Steve pulled his car along side of hers. She had him drop her off at her car because she didn't want him knowing where she lived. The fact that he was a cop and could easily find out where she lived didn't cross her mind.

Steve got out, went to the passenger side and opened the door for her. As she got out he held his arms out for a hug, and she fell into them. The embrace was warm and soft. She could feel his strength. She got a whiff of his cologne, closed her eyes for a second and let herself get lost in the moment.

"I hope you enjoyed yourself," he whispered.

"I did," she said coming out of her trance.

"Can I give you a call?"

"Sure."

Naysia was in her car when he pulled off. She laughed to herself at how giddy she felt. She felt like a second grader all over again. It was a feeling she never thought that she'll get again. She looked forward to having that feeling again. Any man that could make her feel such a way was worth going on another date with.

****

Naysia is from Camden, but lives in Philly. She moved to Philly when P-Hall put her under his wing approximately six years ago. In many ways he up graded her. In Camden it wouldn't have been no way she would have been able to make the kind of money that she was making over there. Dudes were too disrespectful where she was from and only used females for what was between their legs. That's the reason she always came back to the hood to shine on dudes. Every time she came through she was looking good, jumping out of some nice wheels. Nobody out there knew how she got hers, all they knew was at thirty she still looked twenty. Dudes she knew and use to mess with would try to push up but she wouldn't give them any play. She had moved on to better things. She kept a few of her old friends from Camden, even they didn't know exactly what she was into. All they knew was that she messed with some dude from Philly that got money.

CHAPTER 6

EZEL DIDN'T KNOW WHO KILLED THE TWO DUDES ON HIS block. He wasn't feeling any type of way about them. He was more upset about the disrespect of killing somebody on his block. It didn't matter who he was renting it to.

His mans Andy who he was renting the block to was furious. He wanted rec. At first Ezel told him to fall back since they didn't know who did what. He wanted to find out what was going on first. Since everybody was acting like they didn't know what was going on he gave Andy the green light to go in on certain surrounding dope blocks.

Waterloo street was full of people mainly women and children. Lookouts were on both ends of the corner. The dope boys were in the middle of the block trapping. It was also a couple of shooters mingled in chilling with the females. It was one of the most organized blocks. They kept it quiet and the police didn't bother them as much. All that was about to change as the blue maxima slow rolled behind two cars. It had just let two dudes out. One walked on the left side of the street the other went to the other side. Nobody seem to be paying attention, but Bop was on point. It was his job to be. He seen a dude across the street a little over dressed for the nice eighty-degree weather. He had a big coat on with a fur hood over his head. Everything in Bop knew something was wrong. He yelled his manz name real loud. His manz turned around to see Bop pointing his finger at the dude who was heading his way, yet he never bothered to look at dude. He got wide eyed as he zoomed in on dude that had his gun pointed at Bop. Shots rang out, Bop dropped immediately. His manz who he was trying to warn took off running taking a couple of shots to the back. Their shooters came out busting at the two dudes.

It was a brief shoot out but the two dudes made it to their car and the getaway driver peeled off.

****

P-Hall was hurt when he found out that his two comrades had just gotten killed. He heard about the incident right after it occurred. He didn't bother to go to the scene. He didn't want his face to be seen. He knew for sure who had this done.

A few hours later P-Hall received a call from his manz Zaid. "I heard what happened. Some goons came through ma way trying to pull the same stunt. I don't want to get animated on the phone, but I need to polly (Politic) with you."

"No prob, we can make that happen. I'll give you a call."

P-Hall knew if the same dudes that hit his block came through Zaid block then something really was up. A piece of him didn't want to trust Zaid, he could be bullshitting. It was a possibility that he had something to do with it, but that was all wiped out because in his mind he knew exactly who was behind it.

****

Baby-K exited the truck, tucked his gun in the back of his pants, and covered it with his shirt. P-Hall came around from the passenger side as they approached Ezel. It was still two dudes in the Escalade, they stayed behind the tint holding the heavy artillery in case something jumped off.

Ezel and his dudes were in two cars. A Dodge Magnum and a Chrysler. Both of them tinted. Ezel was the only one outside of the car. While walking up Baby-K nor P-Hall could see who the other dudes were because the front windshields were both tinted. One thing they knew was that it was some shooters in there.

Ezel stood in front of his car with his arms folded like he wanted problems. He didn't try to hide the gun on his hip.

Ezel was dark skin, bulky, with big lips, big nose, and a low haircut. He stood about 5'11. Baby-K stood around 6'1, a little bigger, a low hair cut, light skin with no hair on his face. P-Hall stood 5'9, broad shoulders, low cut, with a big beard.

The tension was thick as smoke when they walked up. The vibe was eerie. If this was a cowboy movie the famous western sound would have started playing like it always do when the bad guys enter the bar.

"What up, I thought we had an understanding," Baby-K said standing in front of Ezel.

"I don't know what you talking about, aint that what you told me," Ezel responded sarcastically?

His smart remark confirmed everything for them. Ezel knew exactly what he was doing. Him and Baby-K knew each other well, to the point that even though they were both standing on front of each other not trying to show any emotions they knew what the other was thinking.

"So basically, ma word wasn't good, huh?"

"It aint about ya word. I made ma rounds," Ezel responded. That let P-Hall know that he did do that to Zaid's block.

"I heard."

"I had to let mothafuckas know you can't violate ma shit, and still be eating like I'm some type of pussy. The dudes you had out there aint count anyway. They were ponds." Ezel put on a little smirk like he knew what he said had touched a spot.

Baby-K didn't like the sinister look he got from Ezel. He knew that look Ezel gave when he was trying to play somebody out. Played out was exactly how he was feeling too. Even though he tried not to show it. In the car behind Ezel's car sat two Puerto Rican dudes in the front seat. It was a couple of other dudes in the back seat ready for action. This meeting was taking place about fifteen feet away from a church. Its members started coming out in droves.

"I see I'm wasting ma time," Baby K said.

"You are," Ezel responded as they walked away back to their car. A big smile flashed across his face. Only if one of them would have turned around and saw it.

Baby K hopped in his truck not saying a thing.

"What happened," Chew asked from the back seat? He had the chopper laying across his lap.

"He basically told me fuck me," Baby K said with fury in his eyes.

"Not in them words though," P-Hall corrected.

"It might as well have been in them words. I'ma give em what he want though."

****

Jinger and Trudy were walking through the Franklin Mills Mall about to walk up the stairs when they seen Qadir, and one of his friends.

"So, this where ya'll come to spend all that money them suckas be giving ya'll," Qadir joked with a smile on his face.

"Hey Qadir," Trudy said happy to see him.

Jinger stood there looking at him. He was looking as good as the first day she saw him. Qadir was light skin, slim with waves, and a closely groomed beard that tried to connect.

"Never thought I'll see you here," Trudy said.

"I don't know why not, I got money to spend too. A lot of it," he added looking at Jinger with a smirk. "What's good with you? You were out of control last time I saw you. Whenever I see a chick that's out of control the first thing I think is that some dude not doing his job right."

"How you get that from that night?"

"I'm saying it's true."

Jinger shook her head blushing. She didn't know what else to say.

"You seem like a sweet chick. I'm going to give you ma number so we can get together sometimes." He basically dictated to her what was going to happen. She was kind of glad he did because she liked him but didn't know how to go about it.

Jinger had seen Qadir type of confidence before. It was plenty of dudes from the hood that like to walk around with their chest out talking loud and slick like they were really that dude. Being young she was still trying to weed out the ones that weren't really like that.

She like to categorize the dudes she messed with so she could deal with them accordingly. She had the get money category, the broke, the real, the fake, the bitch, etc...., some of these categories were a mix. No matter how many categories there were they all fell between two, either got money or broke. Her and her friends talked a lot about hood politics, it was their world. Nothing else mattered to them. From the things she heard about Qadir she put him in the money, but dangerous category.

****

Jinger and Qadir kissed uncontrollably as Qadir shut the hotel door. Jinger was all over him, kissing and sucking his face like she was possessed. She was coming on strong, but he matched her aggression. He had her dress up over her waist exposing her thong. He rubbed all over her soft butt, then picked her up and tossed her on the bed. She leaned back on her elbows looking back up at him in shock. He didn't look as strong or aggressive as he was. He came out of his clothes showing her that he was full of surprises, big ones. He grabbed her legs yanking her off the bed. She couldn't believe she was being man handled like she was. She had no control over what was happening. She loved it though. He bent her over the dresser where the TV was, she looked back at him waiting on his next move. Not paying her any mind he caressed her soft, fat, light skin ass. Then reached in her crack pulling out her thong ripping it to the side. He penetrated her wetness then lifted her right leg up making her put her knee on the dresser. She was on her toes with the other leg. She made the sexiest faces and her moans made sweet music as she looked back at him hitting it. A couple of positions and an hour later they were on the bed laying in sweat.

"You wonna taste this," Qadir said about to light the Purple Haze.

Jinger nodded her head yeah. He lit up, took two pulls then passed it to her. She held the dutch in between her fingers with sophistication. It was obvious to Qadir that she was a smoker. Smoking after sex did for her the same that it did for dudes. She just didn't smoke as much.

"You and Jacinica still beefing?"

"I'm not worried about her," Jinger said passing him the Dutch. "She all butt and gut. Don't nobody want her that's why she trying so bad to hold on to her man."

"So, you don't mess with Wade no more?"

"We never really messed with each other like that. We just use to be getting it in. Sometimes I be watching Laquanda's kids for her and he come over do his drug thing or whatever. That's the only time we really get together. I don't know how it even got back to her."

"That's easy, Laquanda," Qadir said like it was obvious. He was thinking that she can't be that bright if she couldn't figure something as simple as that out.

"Do he be taking a lot of drugs over there?"

"He be having them big blocks. What ya'll call them, Bricks? The most I saw him with was like three of them. I don't know how much that stuff is.

I got the drop on that fool and he don't even know it. That'll be a nice come up if I could catch him with some of them things. Qadir was thinking how prices were almost thirty-five thousand at the moment. Jinger had no idea that she was feeding information to one of Wade's enemies. Even though they weren't beefing directly. Wade and Qadir's manz was beefing, which meant Wade and Qadir was beefing. That's just how it goes in the hood. Qadir thought about putting his mans on point, but it was money involved. He figured if he just took care of it himself his mans a take care of him later, plus he'll keep what he got from the jux.

"So, you don't really care about dude?"

"No, he aint my man."

"Let me come through and lay him down then."

"I don't know about all that."

"You said you don't care about him. He aint going to know you had anything to do with it. It's going to be something in it for you too."

Jinger thought about it in doubt. Qadir didn't let her off easy. He kept trying to talk her into it, asking her questions like how often do she baby sit, and do Wade always come through. The rest of the night he treated her special, even putting his face in the pussy on the second go round.

****

Jinger eventually conceded. Two days later she was still having after shocks from the orgasms she had with Qadir. She felt like if all she had to do to keep getting that feeling was set somebody up then she figured she'll be setting a lot of dudes up.

Jinger called Qadir early to let him know that she would be baby sitting for Laquanda. She had partied all weekend. It was a Sunday she didn't have anything to do and she needed some money. Laquanda's kids were already asleep so they weren't going to be a problem. Her baby father was in prison, she was creeping with another dude.

"I'll be back early, like eight in the morning," Laquanda said grabbing her purse off the couch then hooking it around her shoulder. Her keys jiggled on the way out of the house.

Jinger didn't know what to do next. She had told Qadir that she would be there but wasn't sure if Wade would come over. All she knew was sometimes when she was watching Laquanda's kids he would come over and cook up. It was where he handled all his drug business.

A knock on the back door caused Jinger to become nervous. She knew that it was Qadir because she told him told through the back.

"He here yet," he whispered peeking his head in. He came dressed for the occasion, in all black from head to toe.

"Aint nobody here but me and the kids," she said looking at him trying to be sneaky. He tightened up after she told him that he wasn't there.

"When is he supposed to be coming?"

"Told you I don't know if he coming or not."

"You aint call em?"

"I called him, but he might not have what you want with him. Just wait a while, see if he come."

Qadir agreed, he didn't get all prepared for nothing. He kept his gloves on and they kept the lights off. Only the TV was on. They sat there chilling on the couch talking. That lead to her giving him some head then he hit it from the back. Afterwards they sat back on the couch waiting.

After almost two hours Qadir began growing impatient. "Call O'boy," he said tapping her on the thigh.

Not soon after he said that they heard somebody open the screen door and began knocking. Qadir was trying to figure out where to hide. Jinger pointed him to the coat closet. He quickly made his move. Jinger opened the door letting Wade and his friend in.

"What took you so long Wade said walking by her?"

"I was sleeping," Jinger lied.

Wade gave his mans the bag. Dude took it in the kitchen. Wade sat on the couch with Jinger trying to smash as usual.

I know they both strapped. When I move I got to make it count, Qadir thought to himself. He wanted the timing to be perfect. He wasn't trying to chance it with Wade on the couch and his manz in the kitchen. His manz a have too much time to make a move.

"Whats good with you," Wade asked? He gave her a little kiss on the cheek. She didn't think she smelt fresh after having gotten it in with Qadir.

"I don't appreciate what you did to ma girl face. You aint have to do her eye like that. I had to wake up to that mess."

"Tell her to leave me alone then."

Qadir couldn't see Wade's manz. Jinger and Wade were sitting on the couch in front of the closet facing the TV. He could see them clearly through vertical line in the closet door.

"Yo, it aint enough ice," dude came out of the kitchen saying.

As he came back into view Qadir busted out of the closet startling him. Bang! Qadir shot dude in his face, he fell to his knees holding his face. Wade turned around catching a bullet to the side of his head.

Qadir hit both of them a few more times making sure they were finished. Then ran in the kitchen and put everything back in the bag. He came back out pointing the gun at Jinger, she almost jumped out of her skin.

"No, don't kill me. I did everything you said do."

"Chill, I'm not going to kill you. I'ma shot you so nobody a think you had anything to do with it. You're going to be able to sell it better, trust me."

Jinger was thinking that that wasn't part of the plan. He shot her anyway then ran off. She heard the shot and seen him run off but it took a few seconds for her to start feeling the pain.

The cops arrived to a blood bath. Their guns were drawn as they scoped out the house. The tall dark skin cop had seen two dead bodies laying there and the closet door wide open. He pointed the bodies out to his partner and went to check the closest.

"We got a live one over here," his partner yelled.

A few other cops came rushing in. Jinger laid there at the bottom of the steps crying. One of the police officers helped her up.

"Get the medic in here, we got a live one!"

Some how the word had gotten back to Laquanda. She was already outside crying going crazy trying to get in the house. All she wanted to do was get to her kids and make sure they were alright. Soon a police officer brung them out. She hugged and kissed them like she hasn't seen them in years. A minute later Jinger was brung out.

"Its Wade, He's dead," Jinger said with an apologetic face.

Laquanda looked back at her confused. She had no idea Wade was going to be there. Now she was trying to figure out did Jinger do something to him or what. She had questions that she tried to approach the officer with as he came out of the house, but he wouldn't give her any information.

CHAPTER 7

JINGER LEFT THE HOSPITAL THE SAME NIGHT WITH HER MOM and brother. Her injuries weren't serious, but she was still shaken up about what had happened. She told the detectives that a man came there with all black on and had started shooting. She had no idea how much of her story they really believed, all she know was that they took notes and got out of her face.

The next day her friends were showing up at her house happy that she was doing alright. They sat around talking about who could have done it. How Wade had all this beef and dudes was jealous of him. They were going on and on with no idea about what really happened. The fact that their assumptions was so far off the mark put Jinger at ease a little.

****

At the funeral Jacinica and her kids were crying uncontrollably. There were people around consoling them. Laquanda's cries were silent. Jinger wrapped her uninjured arm around her and put her head against hers.

"The lord got em now, he's in a better place," Jinger told Laquanda. She felt like she had to say something. She still felt bad, or she felt like she was supposed to feel bad. She didn't know, she just wanted all this to pass so people could move on. Dudes die every day in Camden, she knew that it wouldn't take long for people to get over it. Until then she had to go through the motions.

Jinger tried her best to avoid Jacinica, but it was inevitable that they run into one another. Jacinica heard all about how Jinger was there when her man got killed. That's why she lost it when she seen her.

"Yooooou," Jacinica said pointing her finger at her.

Jinger was walking down the steps trying to avoid her.

"It's all your fault." Jacinica tried charging towards her but was held back. "No, it's her fault she set him up. I know that bitch had something to do with it," Jacinica kept yelling.

She was being taken the other way, but she had drawn enough attention that people had started giving Jinger the evil eye. Jinger played shocked. Trudy came and put her arm around her and got her out of there. They didn't go to the burial site because of that incident.

Jacinica didn't let go of the notion that Jinger had something to do with Wade's death. She kept throwing it in the air, telling all of Wade's boys. Within a few days the word was that she really did set him up.

Jinger didn't find out how serious it was until one night when they were out at Sofi's, a local bar. It was two months after Wade's death. Jinger was healed up and decided to go out to have a good time with her girls. Her and her girls were getting a lot of love. Dudes hitting on them and buying them drinks. It was like old times. This is what Jinger felt like she was missing. She was in there without any worries. The Wade incident had blown over, so she thought. She sat at the bar sipping her drink, talking to her girls, oblivious of the danger heading her way.

Two dudes from Wade's block was going her way belligerent. They didn't know her but they had been souped up by their manz. The first dude walked through her friends to her, put his hand over her head pointing down at her looking across the bar to his people for confirmation. Everybody around Jinger was looking at dude like he was crazy, wondering what was he doing. Jinger looked up and seen him pointing at her. She reached up to smack his hand, at the same time she tried looking across the bar to find out who he was looking at but once she touched dude he punched her in the face real hard putting her down. All her girls started trying to jump him, but he was chipping them. The other dude shot him some bail. The dudes who the ladies were talking to stood by watching. It was eight chicks fighting two dudes. The girls were trying to get them, even though they had numbers things weren't working out well for them. The girls were getting their hits in, but the dudes were punching them like they were men, folding them. A couple of the two dudes manz tried to get them out of there, but Shay and Fee started tripping on them too. One dude hit fee and her legs buckled, she went right out. People started breaking it up because it was looking bad. The dudes hurried up out of there.

****

"Every time you leave here you come back with something wrong with you. Shouldn't that tell you something," Jinger's mom said handing her an ice pack for her eye.

"Please mom, not right now," Jinger pleaded.

She laid on the couch with her ice pack. The doorbell rang and her mom came out of the kitchen to get it.

"You too," Jinger's mom said seeing that Trudy's face was beat up as well. "What's wrong with ya'll girls. Ladies don't put themselves in positions for stuff like that can happen."

"It wasn't our fault, they started with us," Trudy said.

Jinger's mom shook her head and went back to doing what she was doing in the kitchen.

"You alright."

"Not really, I can't go no where looking like this. Them mothafuckas are some real punks hitting females like that."

"They were Wade's boys. Jacinica got all his boys believing that you set him up. Now they all trying to get at you," Trudy said concerned for her friend. She knew how dangerous his boys were.

"You for real," Jinger asked sitting up. "O ma god, this is some bullshit. I aint have nothing to do with him getting killed. I got shot too."

Jinger became frightened. If Trudy got word of it she figure it must be true. She knew how dudes in the city be knocking each other off, she didn't want to imagine what they'll do to her.

"What am I supposed to do," Jinger asked Trudy looking like she was about to cry?

Trudy felt sorry for her friend. She grabbed her hand and held it. Just fall back. I doubt they try to come in here. I have to find out more of what's going on. We'll come up with something, we aint going to let anything happen to you."

Jinger appreciated her sentiments, but she didn't think she could really do much to save her. Trudy left and Jinger went up stairs to lay down. Feeling doomed she could do nothing but think. *What have I gotten myself into*, she asked herself? She thought about Qadir, how she hasn't seen him since that night. She wallowed in her guilt until she fell asleep.

****

Jinger's mom came in the room waking her up for dinner.

"What time is it," Jinger asked?

"5:45," her mom answered looking at her watch.

Jinger napped way longer than she wanted to. When she got downstairs her mother and brother was already at the table. Her plate was already waiting for her. Her little brother had a big smile on his face. This was his first time seeing her since the fight.

"Who gave you that doudie," he asked laughing.

His mom checked him and he stopped making fun of his sister. Holding back his smile he began eating his food.

"Did you ever send Naysia any of them pictures ya'll took the night of the prom? I forgot to tell you that she said send her some, especially the ones with her in them. You know how much she love herself."

"I have to get them off my phone and send them to her," Jinger responded.

While Jinger and her mom were talking about her aunt an idea came to her mind. After eating she called her aunt."

"Hello."

"Hey Aunt Naysia."

"Hey, what's going on? I'm still waiting for them pictures."

"My mom just told me. I got you. Aunt Naysia I want to come live with you."

"Come live with me, why?"

"I got myself in some trouble that I don't think I'm going to be able to get out of."

"Do it have anything to do with the time you got shot?"

"Yes, dude friends think that I set him up. It's serious, I heard they plan on doing something to me."

The crackling in Jinger's voice let Naysia know how serious it was. Even though she wasn't fond of the idea, she wasn't about to let anything happen to her niece.

"Alright, when do you want me to come get you?"

"Tomorrow if you can, I'll pack all my stuff tonight."

"Did you tell ya mom yet?"

"I'ma tell her as soon as I get off the phone."

"Alright, you do that, and I'll see you tomorrow afternoon."

Jinger didn't know how she was going to bring it up to her mom, or how her mother was going to feel. The good thing was that she was old enough to make her own decisions.

Her mom was lying down when she walked in the room. Jinger sat at the foot of her bed looking at her.

"What is it you want this time," her mom asked knowing the only time she got some quality time from her daughter was when she wanted something.

"I don't want anything. I came to tell you that I'm moving with Aunt Naysia tomorrow."

"You moving out, hallelujah!" Her mom threw her hands up joking. "I thought I was never going to get rid of you."

Jinger enjoyed a laugh with her mom for a second. "For real though mom, I'm out. It aint safe for me in Camden no more."

Seeing that Jinger was serious she asked, "why not?"

"I got mixed up in some dumb stuff."

"I keep telling you Jinger, you know I didn't raise you up like that. You smart, you could go to college and make something of yourself instead of wasting your potential. You want to live the good life so much you have to work for it. You think people who have millions of dollars sit around and that stuff just comes to them? No, they worked for it and are working to keep it. That's what people do in the real world.

Jinger heard her mom talking but really wasn't listening. It was the hundredth time her mom told her that. All she heard was school, work, Labor, job, all words that didn't interest her. The things she wanted them things couldn't provide fast enough and wouldn't provide enough of it. Plus she wouldn't have the freedom to do the things she like doing. She often thought that if a regular job could get her paid then why wasn't you paid mom. They were only thoughts. Those words never came out of her mouth. She didn't want her mother to feel bad. Nobody she knew who lived the life she wanted to live had a regular job. They All got theirs illegally. Comparing their lives to the people she knew who worked all day everyday, the other was much more alluring.

CHAPTER 8

NAYSIA DIDN'T COME TO CAMDEN ALONE, SHE BRUNG TWO dudes with her. When she got out of her Purple Porsche Cayenne they got out of their grey and black Chevy Camaro. They posted up outside of Jinger's house. Jinger came out dragging a bag of clothes.

"That's all you got," Naysia asked on her way in the house.

"No, its more bags in there."

Jinger was amazed that her aunt had a Porsche too. If she would have known that back in when it was prom night she would have wanted to drive that. The over all picture of staying with her aunt became more glamorous.

"You need some help," one of the dudes asked Jinger?

She didn't know that they were with her aunt so she looked at him like he was crazy, and told him, "no".

"Who the guys out there," she asked her aunt when she went back in the house?

"They ma goons, you said it was serious. I brung them in case somebody thought that they were going to be able to get something off. Not if I can help it."

Jinger had no idea how well connected her aunt was, but she still felt secure in her presence. Once all the bags were packed Naysia assured her sister that she would take care of Jinger. Jinger gave her mom a hug and a kiss then they left.

****

Naysia had a nice house in the suburbs. It was twice as big as the town house Jinger was used to in Camden.

"To let you know I'm a clean freak," Naysia said.

Her house was beautifully decorated, adorned with black art, pictures of family and friends, and ornaments. A chandler, expensive furniture, and a spiral staircase among other things. Naysia smiled as she seen her niece looking in awe. This was her first time at Naysia's house.

"I can't believe the whole time you were living like this and left me in the hood with the rats and roaches."

"Ya'll don't have roaches or rats, Aint nothing wrong with ya'll house."

"Yes it is, it don't look like this. This the kinds of house I only see on TV."

"Well you are living in one now. Come on so I can show you ya room."

They put all the bags in the empty back room.

"We could go get you a bedroom set tomorrow."

"Why don't we just go get mines from ma house?"

"I want you to have everything new. It's a fresh start for you. We got a lot of shopping to do anyway. It'll be fun," Naysia said giving her a pat on the shoulder before leaving the room.

Jinger sat on the floor unpacking going through her things. She didn't regret moving because Naysia's crib was unequivocally a better place to live. It was beyond her dreams. She wanted to live that life, but to her that meant nice clothes, shoes, partying, smoking, drinking, and fucking. This was something else, she just hoped it wouldn't be boring. While unpacking she found her prom pictures and took them downstairs to show her aunt.

"I didn't have a chance to get them copied," Jinger said handing them to her. She sat on the couch and they looked at them together.

"Ya'll look so cute together. Is he ya boyfriend?'

"Just friends," Jinger quickly responded.

"Friends with benefits," Naysia asked with a crooked smile. Jinger smiled back. "I know how it go. You can't lie to me."

Jinger was blushing, even though her aunt was young and fly she wasn't used to talking about sex with her. She respected her too much. Naysia gathered all of the pictures up and put them back in the manila envelope. She placed them on the table and turned towards Jinger. "What really happened the night you got shot," she asked?

Jinger looked at the floor shaking her head as if it pained her to even think about it. Naysia rubbed her back for solace. Jinger didn't need to be comforted, she wanted to forget the whole thing. She didn't know how to tell her aunt though.

"I got caught in the mix of a robbery." Jinger said lifting her head up to look her aunt straight in the eyes.

"I know that. That's not what I'm asking. I wonna know did you really have dude set up?"

The question was a little upsetting for Jinger. There was a moment of silence. It wasn't that she didn't trust her aunt, she was just wondering why she would try to get something like that out of her.

"No, if I did I wouldn't tell anybody. You know how it is." She didn't know how it sounded, but when she said it she was looking at her aunt eye to eye.

"It's alright. That's a good answer. You aint suppose to tell nobody nothing like that. You more street smart than I thought. That was a test right there."

That was no test, she really wanted to know Jinger thought to herself.

****

Now what, Jinger asked herself? She sat on the couch scanning the beautiful house. It was so boring that she didn't know what to do. The last couple of days they had been clothes shopping and furniture shopping for her bedroom. She had hooked her bedroom up, but It didn't have that feeling like it was hers.

Naysia told her that she had to make a run and left leaving her by herself. Jinger wasn't a home body. She was wondering was her fear real enough to make such a drastic change. While having them thoughts she heard keys jiggling at the door. Thinking Naysia must have forgotten something she didn't pay it any mind. P-Hall walked through the door like he owned the spot.

"Who you?"

Jinger was startled seeing that it wasn't her aunt.

"I'm Naysia's niece. Who you?"

"P-Hall," he answered. "Where Naysia at?"

"I don't know, she said that she had to go do something."

"You alright here," P-Hall asked before making his way up stairs?

She shook her head yeah then watched him disappear up stairs. She knew by P-Hall's look that he was a straight hood dude. To her he didn't seem like her aunt's type. He wasn't ugly, she just thought that her aunt would have a more sophisticated man. Her aunt had class and Jinger didn't think that his presence matched hers. She felt that only a certain kind of man could tame her aunt.

Despite what her initial thoughts were she noticed he was dripping in ice. That plus he had the keys to the house, he must be getting some type of money. One thing she knew for sure was her aunt wasn't going to settle for a regular dude.

Bored and Nostalgic Jinger picked up the phone and called Trudy.

"Ya'll bitches turn that radio down so I can hear who calling me," Trudy yelled from the back seat.

"Aint like it's somebody important calling you," Fee said turning down the radio.

"Bitch shut up, hello."

"Who you talking to like that?"

"Jinger? Allll, ma girl. What you mean aint nobody calling me of importance. You don't get no more important than my girl." Trudy was extra drunk, and loud. They all were.

"That's her? Let me talk to her," Shay said trying to take the phone from Trudy.

"Hold up," Trudy said yanking it away from her.

"Fuck Jinger, she from Philly now. She could stay her ass over there," Fee blurted out in her drunken voice.

"Who that talking about fuck me?"

"Fee, she drunk acting all stupid. You know how it is. What's up with you though? We miss you already. What it's been like a month?"

"It hasn't even been a week yet."

"It seems longer, you know how tight we are. We used to being together everyday."

"I know right, I miss ya'll too. I'm extra bored out here. I'm not in the hood. My aunt got me out here in the suburbs. I hear all crickets when I step out."

"I couldn't live like that, that's too quiet. I gotta be where it's at."

"What am I missing?"

"Everything, we still doing us. These fools still out here killing each other and acting like they don't want to come up off of nothing. I don't know why they so tight, aint like they going to be alive to spend it all. Might as well pass some on before they get killed, "Shay said giggling to herself."

"That's harsh," Trudy said.

"Yeah well, it's true," Shay stated sternly.

"Did you tell her what I was saying the other day," Laquanda asked?

"O yeah, Laquanda wanted me to let you know that no matter what you her girl. She don't believe you had anything to do with her brother's death. We tried talking to his dudes but they're salty. They need somebody to blame and Jacinica already got in their heads."

After they finish talking Trudy gave Shay the phone. It was like they didn't have as much respect for her conversation with Jinger as they did Trudy's. They got louder and the music got turned up a bit. Jinger heard Trudy tell Laquanda to slow down. The whole time they were on the phone she was wishing she was riding with them.

Drunk, and enjoying the music a little too much Laquanda was going too fast when she tried to make a turn. She turned too wide hitting a curb, losing control, and then hitting a pole. The car flipped and landed on the steps of a house. Jinger heard the whole accident.

"Hello, what happened? Are ya'll alright," she asked repeatedly trying to get an answer?

Something was terribly wrong, she could feel it. After the wreckage there was a brief silence. Jinger was quiet trying to hear what she could. She heard what sounded like movement then screams. Somebody was yelling "help!" Jinger quickly hung up and started calling her friends parents.

Fifteen minutes later she was in a lift on her way back to Camden to see what was going on with her friends.

****

When Naysia came home Jinger wasn't there, she didn't waste anytime wondering where she was. There weren't any stores or anything around for her to go to so she called her cellphone.

"Hello," Jinger answered in a sad voice.

"Where you at?"

"I'm in Camden, my friends were in an accident."

"How did you get there," Naysia asked more concerned about her well being than her friends.

"The lift."

"I'm coming to get you, where you at?"

"At Fee house, down the street from my mom's."

Naysia put down her phone and grabbed her things. "I need you to come with me," she told P-Hall.

"Where we going," he asked looking curious?

"To Camden, I have to go get my niece before something happen to her. Bring ya gun too."

She went to the dresser grabbed a small 9mm handgun and stuffed it into her purse. They left out of there like they were about to go on a mission.

"What type of stuff ya niece into that you gotta worry about something happening to her," P-Hall asked once they got in the car?

"Dudes out here saying she set some boys up to get killed."

"Looking at her I wouldn't have thought that she be on it like that. I guess looks really are deceiving. Ya'll Camden chicks into a little bit of everything."

****

There was a crowd of about thirty people outside of Fee's house grieving. P-Hall's corvette pulled up. Naysia got out in the street and P-Hall proceeded to park. Naysia approached two girls that were leaning on a car.

"Is Jinger out here," She asked?

"She's in the house," one of the girls responded.

The front door was wide open with people going in and out. Naysia looked back at P-Hall, he was posted up against his car with his arms folded. She threw up her index finger letting him know to hold on and went in the house. Jinger sat on the couch rubbing her friend's back trying to console her. She looked up when she felt her aunt standing there staring at her. A sad feeling came over Naysia. The whole scene was sad, but it didn't bother her until she seen the hurt in her own love one's eyes.

Jinger hugged her friend, got up hugged a few more people then walked pass her aunt with her head hanging low. No words were spoken on the ride home. Jinger just stared out the window thinking about her friends. None of them wore seatbelts. Fee died at the scene, everybody else was hurt, but they would survive.

****

Jinger stared at the ceiling in a trance.

"You alright," Naysia asked walking in her room?

"I guess."

"I know what happened to your friends was tragic, but I'm thankful you weren't with them, or I'll be the one in here sad."

"It's just seems like something is happening to everybody I know."

"That's how it is out there, aint nothing but bad decisions being made in the hood. That's why the consequences are so dire. I learned early to detach myself and get out of that box, to go live. Now I don't go to funerals unless it's one of my close friends out there. If I was to go to the funeral for everybody I knew that died I'll have to sleep suited like a fire man. You going to learn, life goes on. Live yours to the fullest."

****

"I don't know what I'ma do with this girl, she too hood to understand. I didn't know how far gone she was until I found out she setting dudes up. That's crazy, I would have never thought that of my niece."

"You really think she did it," P-Hall asked?

"She sneaky, she did something for dudes to want to kill her."

P-Hall sat back listening to Naysia vent, all the while thinking about his own beef which to him was way realer than anything her niece had going on. He had lost another one of his manz the other day. They were getting at each other so much that they had to shut both blocks down. Nobody could get money on either block. If anybody out there even looked like they were trying to trap they were getting sprayed up. Since it wasn't either side only set it didn't hurt them much. They had to shut down because the killing made things too hot.

CHAPTER 9

OVER THE NEXT COUPLE OF WEEKS P-HALL AND JINGER became real fly. She was always at the house when he came over, so they'll be pollying. Their communication wasn't contrived at all, it flowed naturally. He even attended Fee's funeral with her and her aunt. Mainly for back up purposes, in case anybody acted up. They all were strapped up for that occasion, even Jinger. Naysia had given her a little chrome 25. P-Hall had a few hitters outside in a car. In cases when he thought something might go down he always had his hitters around. Turned out they weren't needed, everything went smooth.

Jinger had acclimated into her new living arrangements. She started feeling like she needed to be away from the chaos in order to think better. Plus the up grade felt better. Her aunt would let her use which ever car that she wasn't using and she'll leave the suburbs to explore Philly sometimes making her way back to Camden to chill with her girls, or one of the dudes she was still messing with. Whenever she came back people were on her just because of what she was driving. They thought she was getting some kind of money. Little did they know she was broke.

****

Jinger came in the house with two bags swinging from her arms. Naysia and P-Hall were on the couch watching TV.

"You got something in that bag for me." P-Hall asked?

Naysia who eyes stayed glued to the TV when she came in now had turned towards her. Knowing her niece had sticky fingers she looked at her with curious eyes. Jinger knew exactly what she was thinking. Even though she had told P-Hall how Jinger be on it she didn't want to expose her in front of him so she playfully said, "you was out there shaking your money maker, doing something strange for some change?"

"No, get out of here. My friend brought this for me."

"Let me see what you got," Naysia said taking one of the bags out of her hand. She opened it up pulling out a Prada box. "I like these," she said seeing what else was in the bag. "Ya friend must really like seeing you in nice things. Either that or he got money to blow."

"You can say it's a mixture of both," Jinger said with a big smile on her face.

Naysia played along, but she didn't think Jinger had enough game to pick a dude a part for his riches. Maybe a square, but not a hood dude that was really on his shit.

"That's cute, you should wear this when we go out," Naysia suggested holding up a skirt that looked like it was brought from the kid's department.

"Where we going," Jinger asked unaware that Naysia had plans for them.

"I'll let you know. I don't want to tell you in front of him. He might be a hater and come crash the party."

"As long as you don't come back with a wet ass we good," P-hall said grinning.

"Real funny," Naysia said then got up and went to the kitchen.

Jinger was about to take her clothes upstairs until P-Hall told her to have a seat.

"You like dudes with money? I know one that really got it, I'm talking about its nothing to him. He'll lace you with all that shit you like. The only thing he's not a friend, he's a foe." P-Hall stared into her eyes trying to figure out if she knew where he was going at with this. *My aunt must had told him about what I did in Camden,* she thought while listening. After he finished she didn't say anything, she just looked at him.

"What's up, you wit it?"

"You want me to set him up?"

"I aint going to lie, it aint going to be easy. I want you to get in good with him. I need to know everything you could get me on this dude. I'ma hit you with a rack a week."

"I'm with whatever," she shot back quicker than a jeopardy contestant.

Last time Jinger pulled a stunt like this she got shot so at first she wasn't interested until she heard that rack a week. She jumped on it immediately. She had been wrecking her brain wondering how she was going to make ends meet. Trying to peel the broke dudes she was dealing with was a hassle.

"Alright, I'ma hollah at you later about it. I don't want ya aunt to know about this."

Jinger nodded her head in agreement. They changed the subject before Naysia came back into the room.

****

Ezel wasn't going to be easy, like Baby-K he barely showed his face. His squad was tight, he had dudes in place that took care of things while he enjoyed the finer things in life.

Baby-K knew that it would be hard to catch him in the hood slipping, that's why when P-Hall came to him with his plans he was feeling it.

"I can see that, he a sucka for them young chicks too. I know just where to sick her on him at. She gotta be coming different though. If she on some whore shit he going to dog her out, give her a couple of dollars, and keep it moving."

Baby-K was telling him how to school her. He knew that no matter how bad she was whores get treated like whores. They needed her to find out his movements. Where he stay, play, and hang, cause even though Baby-K, and Ezel grew up together that was years ago. Things changed from then. Now they are older with a lot more money and resources. Since their falling out they knew less about one another than ever.

****

Jinger got ready for what was to be her first day of work, *Shit where am I going to find a job paying me a thousand dollars a week*, she thought while getting ready. She told her mom that she had a real job. She left out the place where she would be working, or the kind of work she would be doing. Still her mom was happy for her.

Jinger anticipated her first day at work being a walk in the park. She had yet to run by a dude that didn't like what he seen when he looked at her.

****

Ezel sat in the laundry mat talking to his Peruvian connect, Pedro. A short harry face guy whom the ordinary person wouldn't suspect ran a multimillion-dollar drug organization. His broken English was carried by a heavy accent native to his country. He was a businessman and conducted himself with such etiquette. At the moment him and Ezel talked and laughed in Spanish.

It was early morning, only a few people were in the laundry mat, none of them knew Spanish so no one understood their conversation. Entering the laundry mat was this beautiful thick red bone catching both of their attention. She had her head wrapped up in a pink and white scarf that ran concurrent with her pink and white flip flops. Her tight pants let her ass jiggle. Pedro took a quick lustful glance that admired her beauty. He didn't chase pussy. He was a family man who already had enough side pieces whom he was taking care of. Ezel had sized her up also. He wasn't a thirsty dude, but when he seen something he liked he just had to have it.

Pedro said something to Ezel in Spanish, Ezel smiled and said something back in agreement. They spoke a few more words before shaking hands then Pedro left.

Ezel seen the young lady having trouble with the machine. Every time she'll put her dollar in the machine it'll spit it back out. He walked over with a hand full of change and started inserting coins loading it up for her.

"Thank you, I only need a dollar twenty-five worth," she said trying to hand him two dollars.

Ezel held his hand up, "you good, this aint about nothing. What's your name?"

"Jinger."

"Jinger," he repeated trying to remember it. "This ma first time seeing you come through here. You just moved around here or something?"

"No, I was staying with ma aunt for a bit. I'm leaving tonight though. I'm just washing clothes before I leave."

"You going back home?"

Jinger nodded her head and gave him this look.

"So, I might not get a chance to see you again, huh?"

Jinger smiled making herself even more personable.

"I don't like the thought of that," Ezel joked. He chatted her up the whole time she was there. He swapped information with her before helping her take her bags to the car.

A piece of cake, she thought to herself waving by to him. For her nothing came easier than getting a guy's attention, even when dressed down like she was.

****

"Hello."

"Everything is in motion. I just have to wait for him to call me."

"Alright, keep me updated."

"What's the plan?"

"Play it sweet and innocent, you know laugh at his corny jokes and all that. You can't be wearing all them tight designer dresses either. You have to tone it down a little. We don't want him to think that you on that type of stuff. Go get something from H and M that look good, but don't cost a lot."

"I got some stuff to wear," Jinger said.

"Act a little shy and inexperienced. You young so you'll get it off. I need you to play the role of ya life. We need him to think he got something different, someone special. Feel me, wifey material. So be on ya best behavior, no hood rat shit."

P-Hall was smiling on the other end of the phone. He knew no matter what a chick did or how she acted that they don't like being called hood rats.

"I aint no hood rat," Jinger said correcting him.

"I know, I'm just saying. Look, I gotta go. Whenever he call you hit me up with an update and we'll put the next move together from there."

P-Hall wanted detailed tabs. He hung up the phone a few seconds after Naysia walked in the room. She felt an awkward energy but pretended everything was everything. P-Hall always kept it real with her that's why she tried not to think much of it. She knew that he had a woman. Since that wasn't an issue everything else was minute, or none of her business. He had a lot going on, she knew she wasn't privy to everything. She walked behind the couch and began rubbing his shoulders.

"I need you to stay away from Philly, it aint safe no more. Make sure you on point for anybody following you too," he said looking up at her.

She leaned in and kissed him on the lips. "Ok", she said. It seemed as if she just nixed what he said off, but she heard him perfectly clear. He was always schooling her, reiterating the same thing over and over again. Nowadays she seems to have things down pack. He had been embedding some good hood principles in her.

"I'ma be out late tonight. Fatimah having a stripper party, I'm taking Jinger there with me."

"If you wanted slong in ya face all you had to do was ask," P-Hall joked looking up at her cheesing.

She lightly shoved his head forward. "I'm not going there for that. I'm going to hang out with my girls." Naysia slid one hand in the front of his shirt rubbing his chest. She started kissing him and nibbling on his face and ear. "You don't like that I'm going to go see strippers," she asked whispering in his ear? She lifted his shirt rubbing his stomach then began unbuttoning his pants.

"If I don't want you to go you won't go."

"Yeah, but I love you," she said.

She was behind the couch bent over him, his manz in her hand stroking it.

"I love you too," he said enjoying the pleasure.

He began kissing and nibbling on her face while she focused on other things. She turned her face towards him so they could kiss. Naysia made her way around the couch and stood in front of him. He stroked his own man while watching her undress. Once everything was off she straddled him and began riding him like a bull but she was lasting way longer than eight seconds at the rodeo.

****

The club wasn't that big how Philly main clubs usually be, but it was nice. It was all females there with about eight male strippers dancing fast to club music. Naysia friends were happy to see her. Fatimah was the first one to greet her. She introduced Jinger to everyone as they mingled. One chick sat in the chair with her legs open as the stripper put his face between her thighs like he was eating the pussy. She began grinding her ass on the chair while making it rain on his head. Dude stop acting like he was eating her out, stood up putting his cock in her face. She acted like she was eating it up. He had a sock on his manz swinging it from side to side smacking her in the face with it.

Naysia was laughing at her friend. Jinger looked in awe at her aunt's friend crazy actions. She thought that her friends were wild, but this was another level.

Naysia reached over to Jinger helping her close her mouth. Jinger started smiling realizing she got caught in a trance. They found some seats and a stripper made his way over to them dancing in front of them, not to anyone in particular. He was performing, humping the floor, and all this other stuff. Then he did like an Usher turn around then slid to Naysia, dancing in front of her. Naysia started laughing at how he did it. She must didn't pull out her money fast enough because he sideway moon walked over to Jinger. She looked at his chiseled sweaty body not knowing what to do. Naysia who now had her money out started flicking off bills on him.

"You a trick," Naysia told Misti who was the friend who was try-ing to eat the stripper's cock.

"What? You had it snowing over there like you was in Magic City somewhere."

"I'm trying to show my niece how we play over here."

"Oh, she trying to be in the big leagues. Bring us another bottle of ciroc. We about to get lit."

Misti's friend walked off to go get the drinks. Some of the girls were standing around talking to the strippers who wasn't dancing. Others were getting danced on while others looked on from a dis-tance. Some ladies were chilling, drinking, and talking.

"You really wonna show her how we play let her stay for the after hour special," Misti suggested.

"We here, we aint going no where."

Misti friend came back with two bottles of ciroc and handed both of them to Misti.

Bout time it was after hours they were wasted. A lot of girls had left, but it was still a nice amount there. Mainly the ones who had experienced the after-hour specials before.

One dude came out ripped up in a man thong with some wrap around glasses like the cyclist be wearing. Jinger giggled because of how funny he looked. He had a chair with him, he put the chair down, and stood in front of it then dropped his man thong. He sat in the chair, and his man stood up stiff. The crowd started getting closer for a better view. The music came on, Genunine's classic Pony. The other stripper came out oiled up wearing a cowboy hat, snaking to the music. He started dancing all over the other stripper, giving him a lappy. Jinger couldn't believe her eyes. *What the hell*, she thought to herself. Then what happened next she wouldn't have ever thought she'll be witnessing.

****

"Can't stay for any more of them after hour specials. That was too much for me," Jinger said leaning back in her seat rubbing her forehead.

Naysia looked at her laughing.

"They were some wild boys. I might not ever see men in the same light after that one," Jinger stated.

That night she found out her aunt was a freak on a whole nother level. Her and her friends were enjoying the show, fascinated. Jinger on the other hand was turned off.

CHAPTER 10

A COUPLE OF DAYS WENT BY AND JINGER NOTICED SHE HASN'T received a call from Ezel. Her first thoughts were was P-Hall still going to pay her. As much as she needed it, she doubted he would since nothing was in the works. As soon as she went downstairs and grabbed the phone P-Hall came down after her.

"Did O boy ever get at you?"

Jinger shook her head no.

"Dam, I don't know what's up," he said thinking to himself. "Did you get his number?"

"Yeah."

"Well, why didn't you call him?"

"I was going to wait a few days. Ladies aint supposed to call guys straight after they get their numbers."

"That's square shit you talking, this the hood. That shit don't apply in our world. Call that mothafucka right now."

"I have to go get the number," she said getting up. She came back downstairs and started dialing his number.

P-Hall was hoping that he picked up. It was ten something in the morning, it was no telling what he could be into at the moment. He stood quietly waiting.

"Hello," Jinger said upon Ezel picking up.

"Who this," he asked?

"It's Jinger."

"Jinger Jinger," he repeated trying to place the name with a face. "Oh alright, I remember you. What's up?"

"You forgot me already. That's why I haven't received a call from you."

"It's not that I forgot about you, I'm a busy man. I be having a lot going on. I was going to wait until I got some free time so I could give you my undivided attention."

"Ya undivided attention, huh? That sounds good. I hope you not one of them guys that talk a good game, but don't ever follow through."

"You dealing with a grown man baby, I don't play games. I can show you better than I can tell you."

If she would have been somebody else he might have been offended, but she was young. He knew she didn't know any better. Still his pride took it as a challenge, he wanted to learn her.

"What he say," P-Hall asked once she ended the conversation?

"He said he going to come get me tonight."

"What time?"

"At eight."

"No matter what, don't give him any pussy on the first date. Remember what I said about playing shy. Act impressed but not enough to give it up. He used to chicks throwing themselves at him."

After P-Hall finished saying everything he wanted to say he went back up stairs. Jinger commenced to calling Trudy like she was doing before he came downstairs. Trudy answered the phone sounding jaunty.

"It sounds like you feeling better," Jinger said.

"Hey ma girl, I am."

"What you doing?"

"Nothing really, just waiting for ma man to come home and treat me like a queen."

"You tried to throw that in there knowing I was going to want to know more." They both started laughing knowing what Jinger said was true. "Alright, who is he?"

"Tye, the one who got us let in the club that night you got in all that mess with Jacinica."

"Oh, I remember him."

"I'm in love Jinger, never felt like this before."

"Dam, he must be dicking you down right. I never heard you say you in love with somebody."

"It's how I'm feeling. He has been here for me while I have been recovering. No dude has ever taken care of me like he does. We really got to know each other. I can't help it I feel like this is real."

"You sound serious. I hope what you got last. I caught ma own big fish. I'm going out with him tonight."

"What's his name?"

"You don't know him. He a Philly boy name Ezel. Well he a man, getting major money."

Jinger didn't know for sure what Ezel was getting she just knew what P-Hall had told her. She also wanted to let her friend know that she had something going on too.

"Yeah, I don't know him. Keep me updated though. Let me know if he got any friends that got it."

"Look at you ready to cheat already. I knew all that stuff you was talking was some BS."

"I'm playing. I'm not cheating on ma baby, he too good to me."

Jinger went on telling her about the crazy night she had last night. Trudy couldn't stop laughing. Jinger was giving her explicit x-rated details.

"Dam, ya aunt and her friends are some super freaks. They're probably into that S and M stuff too."

"I know right. They probably are, they into a lot of things. All these chicks got money though. They were in there making it rain like they were a part of BMF. Besides that other stuff it was alright. They some fly chicks. They had everything in the parking lot. Bentleys, you name it. The cars were probably their dudes but shit I want a man with a Bentley too."

"Messing with them you might run into one."

"You think I'm not," Jinger responded sure of herself.

"That's crazy, you got a whole new team on us."

"Never, hopefully I'ma come chill with ya'll tomorrow. If everything go my way I'll have my own car soon. Right now I got a car, but ma aunt boyfriend had let me use it to do something."

Jinger was talking about if everything went well setting Ezel up. It was something that she looked forward to.

****

Ezel scooped Jinger up in his blue Bentley GT coup with mirror tint. She wasn't sure if it was him. She was standing in front of the house that she wanted him to believe belonged to her aunt when he pulled in front of her. She just looked at her reflection knowing that somebody on the inside was staring back at her.

"You coming or not," he asked after rolling the window down.

She lit up seeing that it was him. She didn't have to say anything, her facial expression told him that she was impressed. Exactly what he expected from her.

He took her to a club where his dudes had it sewed up at. Every male and female spoke to him as he came through. That told Jinger something about his status. People don't normally go out of their way to speak to someone who they consider a nobody. She stayed attached to his hip as he worked his way through the crowd. She noticed that she wasn't seeing any bum chicks like she usually did when she went out. She knew clothes and every female in there was wearing some type of designer. She caught her reflection in the mirror and became insecure. The cheap dress and shoes were embarrassing. She felt out of place. She kept catching chicks looking. She knew they were judging her, thinking she a bum chick. *Fuck it, it's for a purpose. I don't know any of these people*, she thought to herself trying to keep what P-Hall told her in mind. Ezel took her to the V.I.P section where a few of his manz were seated with some ladies. He introduced her and let her have a seat first. It was already bottles of rose at the table. Ezel took the liberty of pouring them both a glass.

"That's ok, I don't drink," Jinger said politely declining the drink.

Ezel took the glass from in front of her and asked would she like anything else to drink?

"Some water".

Ezel manz Sony smiled at how innocent she seemed. The chicks with him were already on their third glass, they were running through bottles of Ace of Spades. That's what Sony had brought for them. He gave Ezel a nod as if he might have something in Jinger. Jinger didn't peep that, but she did peep how one of the girls had rolled her eyes at her. She nixed it off with a smirk. The girl was a Barbie doll, probably 120 pounds and looked like she never had an argument let alone a fight. Just knowing she could beat her was enough for Jinger.

"Look like the whole family here," Ezel said.

"Yeah man, beautiful aint it," Sony responded.

"I would say so."

The club was live but wasn't anybody dancing in the V.I.P section. They were popping bottles and socializing. Dudes kept coming up to Ezel and Sony's table saluting them. It was clear who the big men on campus were. Still Jinger tried to be nonchalant about it all. The truth was that even though she wasn't happy with what she wore she still was on the arm of that dude. All the other chicks knew it that's why they were looking on some hating stuff. It actually made her feel good. In her mind that gave her more status than them.

"Don't tell me that's Green eyes over there with his tongue down that chick mouth like that." Ezel said peeping another one of his manz. "Yeah that's him," he said answering his own question. "Told em that he going to catch herpes if he keep kissing these hoes."

Hearing that Jinger wanted to burst out laughing at the chicks that was with Sony, but she caught herself covering her mouth and nose.

"Excuse me, I have to use the lady's room," she said getting up.

"Sure baby, go ahead." Ezel got out of his seat so she could get by then he sat back down.

"Where you find her at," Sony asked?

"I don't know, I think she found me."

"You might got something there, she seem different. You should put a couple seeds in that. All she need is a little upgrade."

"You getting ahead of yaself. I'm just trying to fuck right now. Its going to take a lot more than her looks for me to keep her around."

"I hear you. I'm just saying it's about time you found something."

"I will when the time is right. I can't just put anything in the crib, these hoes are wretched. They not loyal at all, I can't deal with that. Aint nothing worse than a disloyal broad, you gotta treat them like you'll treat a dude."

Sony nodded his head in agreement. He never thought about it like that. After all these years he was still learning new things about the game. Being Ezel's under boss and a student of the game whenever he learned something he would remember it, or even adjust if needed, fixing his shit along the way.

When Jinger was coming back to the table she caught the attention of Green Eyes who was locked in on her until he seen Ezel get up so she could sit down. He made his way over to their table.

"What's good champ, how long you been here?"

"For a minute, I seen you over there playing kissy face with that chick," Ezel said.

Green Eyes chuckled. "You know me, I'm on all things. But if I would had known you was here I would have came right over."

The whole time he was talking his eyes kept glancing over at Jinger. Even when he tried not to, he couldn't help it. He thought he was god's gift to women and tried to smash every pretty woman he could.

Jinger could tell he was on her. Ezel sensed it too, but every female he went out with was stunning. They always drew attention. He wanted everyone to see him with the baddest chicks, so Green Eyes looking didn't offend, or threaten him at all. If anything it was a compliment.

Ezel didn't see Jinger as Sony seen her. To him she was fresh fruit that he couldn't wait to pluck. After they left the club he went straight to the Ramada. It worked on every other chick, plus when he met her she had on sweatpants and some Mr. Miyagi flip flops. He didn't even have to ask if she ever rode in a Bentley before. He felt like he didn't have to do much to hit, especially if she ever wanted to enjoy his company again.

When they pulled up to the hotel Jinger's energy level changed. She got quiet on him then said, "Ezel I'm sorry, I can't stay with you tonight."

"Why not?"

He looked like he was going to be disappointed at whatever answer she gave so she put her pity me face on. She was young but she wasn't stupid at all. Her manipulation started when she was a baby crying to get what she wanted. She eventually figured out that she could get by on her looks, the sad face that became extra ammo. When that wasn't enough she developed different ways to get what she wanted.

"Because I'm not comfortable, I barely know you."

He looked at her for a few seconds. Her answer seemed sincere. She was right, but he never got that from any other female before. He respected it, plus the way she said it made him think maybe she was different. Another chick would have been eager to get smashed just to stay in the loop.

Jinger held firm giving him direct eye contact. She was relieved when he smiled and nodded his head.

"Alright, we're going to chill and get to know each other."

"I have things to do tomorrow morning. Maybe tomorrow night we can get together again," Jinger suggested.

"I'm with that," Ezel said not wanting to push the issue. He kind of liked the fact that she didn't give in so easy. Secretly he was tired of the same routine. Take a chick out, spend a couple of dollars, smash, maybe give her a couple of dollars, and that was that. It was too easy. He didn't respect it that's why he didn't have a wifey. So far Jinger was different.

"Thanks you for tonight, I'll call you," Jinger said trying to get out of the car.

"Dag, can I get a little kiss," Ezel requested?

She didn't mind that. She leaned in planting a juicy kiss on him. It was a wet peck. She pulled back leaving him in that position stuck, wanting more.

"If I give you too much you're not going to want to leave," she said caressing the side of his face. Then she exited the car.

"Oh you going to tease me like that," he said out the window.

Jinger blew a kiss at him then sashayed towards the house. She looked over her shoulder once smiling back at him. After realizing he wasn't going to get anymore than that he pulled off. When she looked back again he was gone. She turned around and went down the street to her car.

CHAPTER 11

Even though Jinger only went out with Ezel once it has been a week since she first met him. Today was pay day, a stack a week was the deal. She waited patiently. P-Hall only stayed over a couple times a week. She didn't understand but felt that was her Aunt's business not hers. She didn't get into their business, but the more she was around the more it seemed that she was being dragged in it.

****

"You still got that chick on this dude," Baby k asked P-Hall?

"She went out with him last night. I gotta see her today to get the scoop and pay her. Everything in motion, I'll let you know what's going on."

"You sure she qualified, that if shit hit the fan she won't say anything?"

"I'm saying Naysia her aunt. I know where her mom stays so if she know what's best she'll be cool. I think she good though, this aint her first caper."

"Why you say that?"

"She staying with Naysia because dudes in Camden trying to knock her head off for some shit she did. Supposedly she had got somebody robbed and killed."

"This right up her ally. Still while this shit is unfolding we need to make some things happen, this dude coming for ma head I gotta go at his. You think she'll body him?"

"Give me some time, I'll see how she on it."

It was rare P-Hall didn't keep it all the way with his manz, but at that moment in the back of his mind he knew he wasn't about to ask her anything like that. Not only that he didn't know her like that, he wasn't about to let her take him down for a body if she got caught. His thing was to make her job as easy as possible, then when something was about to happen she wouldn't even know it. P-Hall could tell that Baby-K was feeling the pressure of the beef. Things were definitely real, but P-Hall stayed in war mode, ready for anything that came his way.

Baby-K dropped P-Hall off at his car and P-Hall went straight to Naysia's house where Jinger had been waiting. She was on point when he came through the door. First she filled him in on the night with Ezel. Once he realized that she didn't have any useful information he became uninterested. That was until she told him how dude Green Eyes was drooling over her.

"That's another one of his manz," P-Hall said thinking rubbing his chin as if he was the Brain from the cartoon Pinky and The Brain.

"What are you thinking about?"

"Nothing," P-Hall lied nixing his thoughts. He was really thinking maybe he could get something out of Green Eyes, but then decided to stick to the script. He didn't wonna try to do too much. He knew that's when things a start going wrong. He paid Jinger what he promised her and still let her drive his Cadillac.

"It's yours for the time being," he said when she tried to pass him the keys back.

She didn't show how happy she was, but she was elated. It wasn't one of his main cars, nobody knew it was his which was why he let her push it.

****

On the ride to Camden Jinger couldn't help but to wonder why P-Hall acted strange when she mentioned Green Eyes. Now she began to think that it had to be more to him than them Pretty Green Eyes.

She pulled up to Trudy's house. Trudy and Shay was out there waiting, happy to see her. Trudy hopped in the passenger, Shay in the back.

"Okay baller, what dude done let you drive his wheels," Trudy asked?

"This ma peoples, he be looking out for me," Jinger said pulling off.

"And what you be doing for him," Shay asked as if she already knew?

"It's not what you think, he mess with ma aunt. But this dude that I met got it like that. He drives a Bentley and everything.

"For real, see what's up with one of his friends," Shay asked?

"Dam you thirsty. I can't plug you in if you're going to be acting like that. You going to make me look bad, I haven't even gave the dude I'm dealing with any yet. I'm trying to have him thinking I'm some type of good girl."

"He buying that," Trudy asked as if it was a laughing matter?

"He seems to like the chase. Maybe it's true that dudes do like it when they gotta wait for it. I don't know, all I know is that I'm trying to play this one all the way out until he make me wifey. I be dressing down around him, acting all innocent. Ya'll should see me. Last night he took me out and I declined a drink. I told him I didn't drink."

They all began laughing.

"You really over there scheming huh," Trudy said.

"Why not, they don't know us over there. I'll plug ya'll in, but ya'll have to be on it how I'm on it. I aint saying exactly, but ya'll can't be acting how we be acting over here. Once I introduce ya'll its on ya'll from there. All his friends got money so it's nothing to get them to spend. That's what they do."

"I'm with it," Shay said.

"I don't know," Trudy said thinking about her relationship.

"Aint no rush, I'm still trying to get to know these dudes. As I get use to things I'll bring ya'll in. Where Laquanda at?"

"She went to Rahway to visit her baby father," Shay said.

"I know she going to want in. She gotta be tired of them losers she been dealing with," Jinger said as she pulled into the Cherry Hill Mall.

Trudy looked at her friend curiously. Not because of what she said, but because of the nefarious giggle. It was something about it that didn't sit right with her.

Jinger was fully committed to pulling this mission off. It was all she could think about. P-Hall had given her a job and a purpose. She wanted to tell her friends about the whole thing so bad that it was eating her up. Since she couldn't tell them she found another way to bring them in by trying to hook them up. At least they'll be able to share in the experience. Nothing she was doing was worth it if her girls couldn't enjoy it with her. That's how she felt.

****

Naysia went on that date with Steve and that was it. She spent the next few months not answering his calls and hoping he wasn't behind every cop car she saw. The first date she was caught in the moment thinking about seeing him again, but once she really thought about it she wasn't willing to do it. She figured the best thing would be to leave it as that instead of misleading him.

The things she had going on was more important than any man. Plus, it was nothing a man could do that P-Hall wasn't already doing. Her whole lifestyle was an extension of his. She felt in her heart that she wouldn't be anything without him, that's why it wasn't anything that she wouldn't do for him. It's also the reason why it almost crushed her when while going through P-Hall's phone one night she came across Jinger's cellphone number.

"Little grimy bitch," she whispered to herself.

P-Hall who lay in the bed next to her sleep started moving. She looked over at him in disgust, her mind racing. All she could think about was how they had been freaking behind her back. In her house, probably on her bed, or somewhere in the house when she was sleep. The onslaught of scenarios compelled her to get out of bed, away from P-Hall before she busted him in the head with something. That's how mad she was at the moment. Not knowing what to do she went downstairs and sat on the couch with her legs crossed hugging one of the couch pillows tight. Mean facing in the dark, the only light was the rays from the streetlights that shined in through the windows. Tears began rolling down her face. She sniffed catching the snot just as it hit her upper lip. Her heart was aching more than any of her joints ever had before. She began thinking about how for the past six years she had been nothing but good to P-Hall. Giving him her all, staying committed even though he had a girl. Being loyal, doing everything he asked of her because she loved him.

She knew that he be smashing other chicks, but for him to hit her niece that really hurted her. After a half an hour she wiped her tears, got up and went back upstairs with the intentions of laying back down until her cellphone began going off. She was about to cancel the call, but after seeing the number she decided other wise.

"Hello," she answered in a low tone as she walked back down the steps.

"Wow, you finally decided to answer your phone, Steve said. "Did you receive any of my messages?"

"Yeah, I had got them. I'm kind of in a relationship and didn't want to mislead you," Naysia whispered as she sat back on the couch.

"Kind of, huh? Is that why you sound like that?"

"How do I sound?"

"Like you down, plus you said kind of in a relationship. What woman that's happy says she is kind of in a relationship?"

Naysia remained silent.

"Hello, you still there?"

"Yeah, I'm here."

"Am I right?"

"Kind of."

"You and this kind of stuff. What are you doing right now?"

"How about you come outside?"

"You do know it's almost two in the morning, right?"

"I know, what better time to chill and enjoy the elements than at night when it's nobody out. Plus, I just want to see you. It's been a while. I been looking forward to seeing your beautiful face again ever since our little date."

He sweet talked Naysia into consenting to meet up with him. She found his words comforting, exactly what she needed at the moment. Beside that she felt like she needed to get out of the house, if not for anything other then some fresh air.

Naysia pulled over in front of a clothing store. It was a spot she knew nobody she knew would be riding through at two in the morning. Steve walked over to the driver side door as she parked. She got out of the car and he wrapped his arms around her giving her the warmest embrace that she ever felt. Even though it was unexpected she enjoyed it hugging him back.

"Dam, you as beautiful as the first time I saw you."

She didn't know how to respond to that. She knew she looked good, but she never had a man tell her with so much passion and conviction in his voice. They say the eyes never lie, as she stared into his eyes she could tell that he meant every word.

For the first time in a long time she felt wanted. Being number two in P-Hall's world she barely felt wanted. Used, maybe needed sometimes, but only when he needed her to do something that had something to do with drugs or money.

"So what's up," he asked as they stood outside of her car. They were no longer hugged up but he leaned up against the hood of her car, still holding her hands as she stood in front of him. His gaze was welcomed by her look of vulnerability.

"Who did it, where they at? Whatever it is I'll take care of it. I'm a cop remember," he said smiling pointing to his badge. "We save the world, this my superman suit, you my Lois Lane. Now what's wrong?"

Him joking brung a smile to Naysia's face making her feel a little better. "Nothing, I'm just not feeling good," she lied.

"Come on now, I can tell you got something on ya mind. If you don't want to talk about it that's cool. I just want you to know I'm here for you if you need me. Sometimes it's good to get things off your chest, or find other ways to forget about them," he said bringing her closer to him.

Again she found herself in his arms. She didn't know why she felt so comfortable there, but she was. She didn't know if it was because he was a cop, or because she was vulnerable. Steve was looking down at her as he talked and gave her a little kiss on the nose, sending a tickle up her spine. She liked it. She lifted her head up a little so he could plant one on her lips, which he did. She smiled caught in the moment.

"Are you working third shift now?"

"Yup, that's why I called you so late. I didn't think you were going to answer, guess I lucked up. Can I see you tonight?"

"You see me now."

"I know, but I'm talking dinner at my place before I go to work. What you think? I'm going to chef something up for us."

"You cook?"

"What, I do it all," he responded?

Caught in the moment she agreed. It wasn't until she was driving that she asked herself what was she doing, but then as she got closer to her house it all came back to her that P-Hall and Jinger was getting it in on the low. She quietly opened the door thinking how the idea thing would be to catch them in the act, so they couldn't deny it if they wanted to.

She tried creeping in case she was to catch anything, but as she walked through the house it was quiet. P-Hall was still sound asleep. She switched back into her night clothes and eased back in bed under the covers like she never left.

As usual when he stayed the night P-Hall left before sun rise. Naysia overslept waking up around eleven. Slightly depressed she wanted to stay in bed all day, but she also wanted to act normal like she didn't know anything. She was still contemplating the idea of confronting them but haven't worked up the courage yet. Plus, while she was convinced, she wasn't 100% sure.

She walked downstairs and became disgusted at what she saw. Jinger walking around with her big booty busting out of her silver pajama pants, and a white shirt that squeezed her allowing her nipples to protrude. Naysia kept her thoughts to herself, walking by without saying her usual good morning.

"It's some eggs and French toast in there if you're hungry."

Naysia kept walking, Jinger didn't think much of it, but when she came back downstairs Naysia was eating cereal.

"Why didn't you get some eggs," Jinger asked?

"Because I didn't want any eggs," Naysia responded in a stern tone.

That caught Jinger off guard, her and her aunt never was in a confrontation with each other.

"Excuse me, guess you woke up on the wrong side of the bed this morning," Jinger said walking off.

Naysia bit her tongue, she really wanted to say something. A response would have led to her punching Jinger in the face, so she just rolled her eyes, and continued eating.

Just so happen Jinger decided to make today one of her in house days, so most of the day the house was quiet as a library. Both of them playing their room trying to avoid one another.

At quarter to seven Naysia left the house in a tight dress, some red bottoms, and a Louis Vuitton bag. When she got outside of the house that Steve had given her the address to she called him to make sure she had it right.

"Yeah, I see you. See me waving," he asked?

She seen him waving and pulled her Porsche behind a black Mazda. Steve had a nice little house on the out skirts of Philly. He greeted her at the door with a hug and a kiss on the cheek, very gentleman like. For a second she thought maybe she could get use to being treated like that.

"Are you feeling better today?"

"I am now," she said.

"I'm glad I could have that effect on you," he said letting her in.

His hands never let loose of her, only going from her waist to the small of her back as he guided her in. Thinking about how sexy she looked in that dress made him want her bad. He felt like he had to be careful though, now that he had a second chance he didn't want to mess it up. She already proved that she didn't need him when she wasn't answering his calls. He didn't respect that she had a situation, he knew that she wasn't being treated right. The fact that she was at his house was proof. The tricky part for him was trying to get to know someone that seemed so elusive. One wrong move and he might not see her again.

"It smells good in here," she said as he led her to the dining room table.

"Thanks, I put a lot of love into it. I hope you enjoy," he said pulling a chair out for her.

Instead of sitting across from her he pulled out the next chair so he could be closer to her. She smiled looking at the delectable three course meal he put together for them. Tuckey meatloaf, mash potatoes, and peas. His efforts didn't go unnoticed.

"You like wine," he asked pouring them a glass.

She nodded her head yes and they toasted to the moment. While eating they laughed and joke, keeping everything basic, nothing personal. Just trying to enjoy each others company. All the while Steve could tell that she was going through something. Any other female would have been came out and told him something, but Naysia was a tough cookie. A different kind of woman, he could tell. That's why he wasn't trying to mess up the moment, she seemed to be enjoying herself. He thought of another way to get it out of her.

The food was finished, Naysia was still laughing. She couldn't help how giddy she felt. It was the complete opposite of her usual self. Steve stared at her with lust in his eyes. He reached out and took her by the hand and began caressing it. Naysia's laughter turned into her blushing like a shy little girl.

"You deserved to be appreciated, I want the honor of being the guy who does it." He gently pulled her out of her seat towards him. She was saucy from the wine, but by the way she looked at him he knew that he had her.

"You don't even know me," she responded.

"I'm a man that knows what he wants and right now I want you more than anything in the world. Everything else a come later," He said as he kissed her lips.

His first kiss met a set of unprepared lips, but when he went back in she was ready, wrapping her arms around him. They French kissed one another to the couch leaving a trail of clothing along the way. She was willing to let him have all of her for the night.

"Umm, this thing soaking wet," he said penetrating her.

Naysia moaned, they gazed into one another eyes, and began kissing again. They made love on that couch for over an hour, but it seemed like all night. Steve took his time and showed her how he would appreciate every part of her body.

CHAPTER 12

WHEN JINGER LEFT THE HOUSE IT WAS EMPTY. NAYSIA DIDN'T come home last night, and Jinger wasn't missing her not one bit. Mainly because of the negative energy she was carrying with her, but she hoped that whatever she was dealing with that she had went to go handle it so she could come back feeling better.

While driving Jinger received a call from Brah, it was unexpected. She hadn't thought about him in months. He wanted to get up, but she couldn't.

"I'll call you later, I'm going somewhere," she said.

"You told me that last time, and I didn't hear anything from you."

"I did call you last time. Your mom said, you wasn't home," she lied?

The pitiful thought that he still lived with his mom turned her off. She had up graded, it was no way that she was going back. She immediately ended the conversation.

"I have to go."

Click!

Jinger never acted like that towards Brah, she just wasn't beat at the moment. Ezel had told her he had something for her. She didn't know what it was, but she was excited to find out.

She arrived at the laundry mat dressed down in some tight blue jeans and a white and black Old Navy shirt. Ezel seen her and smiled as if she brightened his day. One look over and he knew that he was about to do the right thing. He seen a lot of potential in her. The way she carried herself made her different, he liked that. Only if she would be his he could turn her into something special.

The warm embrace said that they were growing more familiar with each other. She could sense that by holding out that she had gained his respect.

"I know I told you I had something for you, but not exactly. I wonna take you shopping. A day out we just throw stuff in the bag, afterwards chill. You don't have to dig in ya pocket for anything though, I got you," he said understating his intentions.

That's even better Jinger thought to herself, but outwardly she acted modest.

"Ezel, you don't have to buy me anything. I'll just go to hang out with you."

"You sure?"

Fuck no, she thought. "Yeah, I'll go," she said in her sweet little gullible voice. In the back of her mind she was hoping she didn't just talk herself out of a shopping spree. She wanted to kick herself in the ass when he left it as that. She felt like she was taking the nice girl role way too far. The goal was to get what she could out of him while doing what she was doing for P-Hall.

****

Jinger had never seen some one spend so much money at once. According to her estimate he had spent about ten thousand dollars on clothes. After paying the cashier Ezel handed Jinger another bag adding to the two she already carried. He picked up his bags, and they exited the store.

"We're going to put these in the car and get something to eat."

South Street was jumping as usual, it wouldn't be unlikely for Jinger to see someone she knew. Her and her girls knew these stores well. After putting the bags in the car they went to the pizza shop. While standing there Ezel thought about how he had to up grade her. *She looked good, but she could look better* he thought to himself.

After eating he took her to a boutique. Jinger had been there before but acted like she hadn't. She acted in awe of everything he wanted her to try on. He watched as she dazzled him. She made everything she tried on come a live. Every time she put something on she would ask him did he like it as if it was for his eyes only. Each time he would tell her he loved it.

"Them dresses wasn't made for anybody else, but you."

Jinger looked in the mirror, she could see him staring at her. She turned around sagging her head.

"This ain't me, I could never afford to wear stuff like this continuously," she said in a low tone.

At that moment he saw how low her self esteem was. He stood up behind her putting his hands on her shoulders.

"This is you Jinger, trust me when I tell you. Look." He was up on her close from the back. "Do you see what I see?"

Of course she was seeing what he seen, but she shrugged her shoulders like she didn't know. She wanted to know where he was going with this.

"Do you see that man behind you? He's a winner." When he started talking about himself she was glad she hadn't said anything, she would have had it all wrong. She thought some up-lifting compliments were going to come her way, but he kept going on about himself. "And when you deal with a winner this kind of stuff becomes you. Get use to the finer things in life."

"Did you fine anything you like maim," the lady asked when she came back?

"We'll take everything," Ezel said.

Jinger couldn't believe that he was going to buy everything. He paid just as much for her things as he did for his. On the inside she was smiling while trying to remain humble. *I finally got a dude that really got it. I'ma ride this thing till the wheels fall off.*

****

While watching the movie Ezel kept talking in Jinger's ear. That turned into a kiss and led to him fondling her. From her breast to her pussy, she allowed his hands to roam her body.

"My dick hard as hell, you might as well let me hit right here."
Jinger responded with a kiss. He grabbed her hand and put it on
his man. Now she was doing the fondling. The theater was dark. They
had the last row all the way to the wall. Ezel stood up in front of her.
Jinger started sucking him off. No one else was seated in the back two
rows. While he was enjoying her head it wasn't enough, he wanted
some pussy. He stopped, stood her up, and started pulling her pants
down. They were so tight he only got them halfway pass her thighs.
That was good enough for him. The movie theater seats were recliners,
so he laid her down threw her legs up and began going in.

∗∗∗∗

Jinger felt good about how things were going with Ezel so far. She
stood in her room with all her new clothes laid out on the bed. A dude
with money that knows how to treat a lady, can't beat that she thought
while matching sets figuring what she was going to wear first. After
hanging her clothes up she called Ezel.
"Yo, he answered?"
"Were you asleep?"
"I'm whining down, why?"
"I just wanted to thank you for such an amazing night."
"It was ma pleasure baby. You fucking with a boss now. Shit like
that is the norm so get use to it, all right?"
"Okay."
"Now let me get some sleep. I got a busy day tomorrow, all right?"
"All right, bye bye."
Before Jinger could get the bye all the way out she heard the phone
click. She didn't care if he heard her say bye or not, she was too excited.
She felt like she had found a gold mine.

∗∗∗∗

The next day Jinger woke up to the sound of P-Hall's voice. He sat on
the side of her bed.

"What's up, what happened last night?"

Naysia came out of the bathroom walking pass Jinger's room. She heard voices, the first thing she thought was P-Hall is in there. She went to her room to check because he was in there before she went to the bathroom. "Just like I thought, they aint going to play me out in my house while I'm here," she mumbled to herself while reaching in her drawer for her gun. She got it and headed straight to Jinger's room.

The door swung open banging into the wall. P-Hall looked up at Naysia like she had lost her mind, he didn't bother to move from the edge of the bed. Jinger was sitting up but still under the cover. Naysia walked came in with the gun pointed at P-Hall's face.

"Ya'll think ya'll going to keep playing me out in ma house, fuck that!"

When Jinger saw the gun she rolled out of bed still trying to hold on to the covers. Doing so her underwear became exposed making things look worse than what it was. Jinger was scared to death, she knew what it felt like to be shot, that's the last thing she wanted to feel again.

P-Hall stood up, and Naysia held the gun pointed at his chest. "What the fuck are you doing?"

"You fucking my niece, I should shoot the shit out of you," Naysia said with tears coming down her face.

"Give me that gun and come here. You don't know what you're talking about."

She was close enough that if he wanted he could have sidestepped and knocked her out but that was his baby. He wouldn't do anything like that to her. He knew she really wasn't going to shoot him.

"Come on, give me that gun," he said reaching for it.

She held it with two hands, tears still rolling down her face. Jinger was on the floor on the other side of the bed peeking trying to see what was happening. P-Hall moved the gun off him and slowly began taking it out of her hands. Once he got it from her he grabbed her towards him. She buried her head in his chest as they hugged.

Naysia held him tight crying. Jinger came from behind the bed still scared. P-Hall looked at her shaking his head. Him and Naysia sat on the bed together.

"What's with you," he asked wiping away tears that were rolling down her face.

Naysia was hurt, it was hard for her to say what was on her mind. When she did Jinger finally realized why she had been tripping on her for the past few days.

"I do a lot of fucked up shit on them streets, but I would never do you like that. Next time come talk to me before you start acting stupid. I had Jinger helping me with some things, that's all." P-Hall explained everything right then and there. "You wasn't supposed to find out about any of this," he said afterwards.

Naysia had a blank stare on her face. Her eyes bounced back and forth between the two of them. She closed her eyes, shook her head, got up, and left the room in disappointment.

"I got her," P-Hall told Jinger and followed Naysia out of the room.

Naysia was lying in bed when he walked in, "You believe me, right?"

"Uhmm hum."

"For real, I aint bullshitting."

"Why would you have my niece doing that?"

"She good Naysia, all she doing is trying to find out some info for me."

"What if something happens to her? Then it's going to be on me."

"I got this, trust me," P-Hall tried to assure her.

Naysia thought about it for a moment, then smirked telling him that he almost got shot. "It would have been ya fault too."

"You was really going to shoot me," he asked smiling playfully jumping on her?

Their serious ordeal turned into a playful moment with P-Hall trying to lighten the mood.

****

Later that night Jinger heard two taps on her room door. "Come in," she said. Naysia peeked her head in then entered all the way. Jinger sat on the bed with all the little cotton things between her toes polishing them.

"I wanted to apologize for earlier. I feel bad that I even thought you'll do something like that to me."

Jinger stopped what she was doing to let her aunt know that she accepted her apology. They hugged and had a moment. Naysia started asking questions about what they had going on with dude. Turns out Naysia knew Ezel, he use to mess with one of her friends. She left that out, but she knew firsthand how dangerous it was for Jinger to be playing with someone like him.

"Are you sure you want to be doing something like this? He aint no small-time dude. He been known to kill a few dudes."

"I'm more than sure. I only have to give P-Hall information, that's easy. Everything I see and hear I tell em. Mean while I'ma try to get what I can off dude.

Bout time something happens to him I should be good. Hopefully I got a nice bag by then," she said sounding like it was nothing.

Naysia never realized how cold her niece was. That moment let her know how little she knew about Jinger. Her lovely niece with the most adorable smile and the little chubby cheeks had grown up so fast she hadn't noticed. Camden had raped her of her innocents, and she didn't know it but Naysia was seeing it. The difference between them was that Naysia wasn't a naïve young girl. She knew how the streets worked and the consequences behind ones actions. She didn't think Jinger understood that part. She tried giving her a little advice about how to move with Ezel. While Jinger listened Naysia could see her words were going in one ear and out the other.

CHAPTER 13

P-Hall pulled up to Cortina's house, his manz John John stood outside of the car while he walked up to the house. They had to be on point at all times. Cortina answered the door disappointed, the last thing she wanted to see was somebody from the life she was trying to leave behind. Cortina was an ex dope fiend who went to rehab and was still in the process of getting her life back on track.

"What's good Cortina?"

"Hey P-Hall, I'ma need a little more time to get that for you."

Cortina thought he was coming to ask about the couple of dollars she owed him from the time he was on the block talking to Bop and she came through needing a fix but didn't have any money. She was looking real sick, and because he knew her he didn't like seeing her like that. That was like eight months ago before she had went to rehab. He had forgotten all about that.

"I aint worried about that, I need a favor."

"What is it?"

"I need you to act like ma little cousin's mom. You don't have to do anything. She just needs to be seen leaving this house a couple times a week. That's all, I'ma look out for you each time. You don't have to worry about that other stuff."

Cortina agreed, and he gave her two hundred dollars.

A couple days ago Jinger had let Him know that she couldn't keep acting like she was coming out of that same house. She didn't know any of the people there and if they were to catch her on their property while Ezel was there that could give the whole thing up.

P-Hall knew she was right. Plus he knew Ezel wasn't stupid. He might all of a sudden start wondering why he never seen her go in and out of the crib, only standing in front of it. It was too late to find her an apartment, so he found the next best thing, a fiend house. Getting a house was the easy part, continuing on with this façade would be a test of time. Depending on how good Jinger played her part. He didn't expect major results right away, he thought of it more as a long-term mission. Unless, and it was a big unless because even though he told himself he wasn't going to ask her before it kept crossing his mind. If she did it that would get the job done and save him a lot of time and money. If she did it, that was the thing.

****

Everywhere P-Hall went he had a shooter for back up. Both sides knew it was S.O.S [Shoot on site], but things had to get done and P-hall had to make sure they was running right. Being on point was second nature, so him and his manz John John rode through the city strapped like it was nothing.

When they arrived at the dope house a big brown bald-headed dude opened the door holding an AK-47. He greeted them with a head nod. Five females were standing at the living room table naked with gloves and a mask on bagging up dope. Another big dude sat on the stool watching them like a hawk. The AK he held wasn't for them though, it was in case anybody tried to rob the spot. P-Hall's visit was a surprise, he didn't show it though. He wasn't one to show emotions. P-Hall barely visited the dope house unless it was important. The importance of this visit was to show John John how everything was supposed to go since he was going to be the new pick up man.

"This John John, he going to be picking up from now on," P-Hall told big man sitting on the stool.

Big man nodded his head in acknowledgement while looking at John John. They were on the same team but haven't met one another until that moment. Everybody had a position to play and everything was on a need to know basis.

While P-Hall was talking to big man John John's eyes kept sliding over to the ladies.

"You sure you're going to be able to handle this," P-Hall asked after noticing it. He couldn't have any tender dick dudes being distracted trying to fuck the bag up girls.

"Yeah, I can handle it," John John responded.

He took that as a pull up. P-Hall knew he could handle it other wise he wouldn't be there.

"You got something ready for us now?"

"Yeah," big man replied and went to grab a bag. "It's 300 bundles," he said handing it to P-Hall. P-Hall handed the bag to John John before they left.

****

The whole ordeal weighed heavy on Naysia's mind. P-Hall and Jinger brushed it off like it was something light, but Naysia was thinking of worse case scenarios. She knew all about P-Hall's beef, how Bop and others had gotten killed. For him to put her niece in the middle of that kind of situation didn't sit well with her. She was responsible for her. She was going to be the one to have to face her sister and live with it if anything went wrong. Would if one of P-Hall's enemies found out they were related. She knew Jinger was too naïve to see that far, all she seen was dollar signs.

Naysia who usually trusted P-Hall's decision making knew that this was wrong on every level. She didn't express how she felt anymore after that day, but they could feel it without her saying anything. They would only discuss things when she wasn't around to keep her from worrying.

Naysia sat in her car reading the text she had just received from Steve.

"Really missing you babe. When you get the chance, I'll love to hear from you."

Dam, he relentless, she thought to herself. She had been ignoring his calls since that lovely night they hooked up. While it felt good at the time, it was something she regretted. She only did it under the assumption that P-Hall was smashing her niece. Now she didn't want anything to do with Steve and was hoping that he'll lose her number before he got her in trouble.

Not long after Naysia blew her horn Brandy came out holding her five-year-old son's hand.

"O my god, He's so cute," Naysia said watching her strap him into the car seat. Little Fuquan just looked at her. Once he was safely strapped in they headed out to the mall.

"Dam girl, we have to start hanging out how we use to."

"I know," Naysia responded. "You be doing the family thing now. It's hard getting you out the house."

"You right, things have changed for me. I don't be wanting to be away from my baby. Plus you know his dad never home, then when he is it's like I got two kids."

"I can imagine. Sometimes P-Hall be getting on my nerves so much I be kind of happy that he don't stay with me."

"You don't mean that. I know you get lonely when you alone in that big ol bed by yourself. You know like I know aint nothing like waking up to a stiff one." They both started laughing. "Did you ever talk to him about leaving his girl?"

"I do, but I can't complain when I'm living like this."

"That's how they keep us on the hook, with their money. I had been peeped that when I was messing with Ezel, he didn't even use to be on no b.s. I just found myself afraid to speak up and have a say about certain things because I didn't want to lose him or anything he provided. That's why once I found another dude that had it and that was into me, I started pushing for him to commit. Once I realized he wasn't I moved on to someone who would. I know you know that you deserve better than sloppy seconds," Brandy said looking at Naysia while she drove.

"I know I know, see you got me feeling all bad and stuff."

"Because you know I'm right. I know you want some kids."

Brandy kept talking, Naysia was paying attention to her rearview mirror. She saw a cop car speeding up from a distance. Usually she'll be on point for other reasons, but lately everyone she seen had her thinking about Steve. She didn't think it was him since he told her that he was working third shift now. The red light allowed the cop to catch up. She lightly shook her head seeing that it was him. Her mood changed to one less pleasant.

"You alright," Brandy asked? She saw Naysia keep looking in the rearview mirror and turned around to see at what. "He aint worried about us," She said turning back around. The light turned green, she crossed the intersection, and Steve turned on the sirens. "I guess he was worried about us, ma bad." Naysia signed as she pulled over. "You don't have anything on you, right?"

"No, we good."

Steve walked up to her car and tapped on the window. He waved for her to get out of the car. Brandy mouth gaped as Naysia exited the vehicle, she could tell that this wasn't a regular traffic stop.

"You doing this again," Steve asked because she haven't been responding to his text or calls?

"I told you I'm in a relationship Steve."

"You said you're kind of in a relationship, He's obviously not treating you right." He tried to put his hand on her waist.

"I can't do this right now," she said stepping out of his grasp.

Steve looked in the car at Brandy who was looking at them wishing she could hear their conversation, but since the windows were up she couldn't. He waved at her, she gave him a half smile and sat back in her seat.

"Naysia, I aint going to hold you, I'm in love with you. I think you feel the same way."

"It's not good timing," she said grabbing the car door handle.

"But you do feel it, right?"

"I don't want to talk about it right now."

"Can I call you then, I'ma call you anyway," he said as she got back in the car.

She shook her head in disbelief as she drove off.

For him when she said it's not the right timing let him know that she was feeling how he was feeling. In his mind if she was feeling how he was feeling then they belonged together.

"I didn't take you for one who like guys in uniforms."

"I don't, but sometimes nature takes its course. Now I can't get rid of him."

"That's what happens when you feed stray animals, they keep coming back."

CHAPTER 14

Jinger was in the house talking to Cortina when Ezel beeped his horn. She came out looking stunning in a blue Alexandria McQueen dress and some Jimmy Cho shoes. Ezel smiled admiring his work. Any female that was going to be with him was going to be looking good and have the best on. Just like his clothes, his crib, his jewels, and his cars said everything about him. The lady that was with him said something about him too. She represented his exclusive taste and style. Not just the way she looked because a good looking woman was a dime a dozen, everything about her had to be right.

If he had known anybody from Philly that had Jinger he wouldn't have been investing his time, energy, or money in her. Not only because he felt like if she dealt with losers then she didn't deserve to deal with a winner like him, but mainly because she could be trying to line him up to be either robbed or killed. He was smarter than that, which was always the difference from a broke dude and a dude who was getting money.

"Jinger do you think that you're a trustworthy person," Ezel asked?

"Yes, why you ask that?"

"I need to know because the kind of things I'm into I need people around me I can trust. I got trust issues, that's why I don't usually do the relationship thing. You seem different though."

"If you don't do relationships how do you describe your relationships with females?"

"Just messing with them."

Jinger pretended to be upset. She faced forward staring out the window as he drove. Noticing a change in her mood he asked, "What's wrong?"

"Here I am falling for you, thinking that you're really into me, come to find out you just messing with me."

"Nah Jinger, it aint like that."

"I hope not because ma mom didn't raise me to be taken advantage of."

"Calm down, I'm not trying to take advantage of you. That's what I was saying, I want something different with you, but love and loyalty is important to me. I'm a different kind of dude. A lot of dudes be on some sucka shit when it comes to their ladies. Me I'll treat a chick how I'll treat a dude if she cross me. If she lie to me or whatever I'ma cut her off. I'm different, certain principles govern my life. I stick to them no matter what. That's why I'm in the position I'm in."

Jinger seen the seriousness in his face as he spoke. He occasionally glanced over at her to see how she was taking things. Even though he didn't care, he was making his position known,

"I just want to let you know. Give you a chance to know the kind of person you're dealing with."

"Ezel," Jinger started saying in her soft voice. "If I'm going to be with you I'm going to be with you alone. You don't have to worry about anybody else, that's not how I am."

"That's what I like to hear. I'ma hold you to that," he said looking at her. She reached out putting her hand on top of the one he had on the middle counseled. He turned his hand over holding hers.

They pulled up to the club and walked in like they owned the place. From the dress to hopping out of the Bentley, to sitting at the table with Ezel and his friends. It all made Jinger feel like her dreams had come true. Like she finally made it. She was loving the moment.

They were attending a going away party for one of Ezel's friends. Ladies were every where. Jinger peeped two of Naysia's friends from the night with the strippers. She couldn't remember their names, but definitely remembered their faces.

One of Ezel's manz poured him and Jinger some Rose. He put a glass in front of Jinger and a glass in front of Ezel. Jinger's first instinct was to grab the glass, but she caught herself.

"She don't drink," Ezel told his manz.

"Ma bad bro," he said reaching to take the glass back.

"Leave it, I got it. Bring a bottle of water."

He had no idea how bad she wanted that drink. She stuck to the script though.

"Ice, to you ma dude," Ezel said holding up his glass. I wish it was more stand up dudes like you instead of these fuck boys always snitching. We going to hold you up. Money, visits, flicks, food packages, phone all-day, you name it. You going to be lamping how only the real is supposed to."

Ezel was standing holding his glass up while talking. Ice was seated across the table holding his glass up smiling, eyes low saucy from all the drinks he had. After almost three years on bail the time had come for him to turn himself in. The last thing he wanted to do was leave the good life, but he felt like he came off with the plea bargain his lawyer had got him. A fifteen with a seven. Do seven see parole, hopefully get a date. Even if he had to do a few more, it was nothing compared to the numbers a lot of dudes he knew had got.

In the hood nobody looked at their situation alone. They always looked at the other situations to make them feel better about theirs. He knew dudes doing 30, 50, even life, who would spend all those years fighting to get back on an appeal. Most wouldn't so he looked at his time like a vacation. He wasn't even going to put in an appeal. He was going to thug his shit out.

Jinger was feeling the atmosphere. Everyone was getting along. The bottles were flowing. The smell of weed in the air, the music blaring, they definitely knew how to party. The only thing she wished was that she could be as saucy as everybody else. This was the kind of environment she liked. She found herself moving around conversing with people. On her way back to her table she ran into Green Eyes.

"What's good Jinger," he said cutting her off?

"Oh hey ahhh....," she was trying to remember his name.

"Green Eyes," he said helping her out.

"I'm sorry, hey Green Eyes."

"Don't worry about it. I know you got some friends, sisters, or cousins. You pretty ladies don't travel alone."

"Green Eyes, every time I see you you're entertaining a lady. I doubt if you need any help in that department."

Green Eyes blushed, flattered. "I don't need help finding a woman, I need help finding that special woman. You know that's like trying to find a needle in a haystack."

"I'ma see what I can do."

"Just bring her around, I'll do the rest."

"You see Green Eyes over there trying to chat up the broad that came with you," Sony said nodding in the direction where they were.

"That's ma dude, he know better."

Sony was skeptical of everything and everybody. Even though he dealt with Green Eyes that was really Ezel's manz. Ezel had been selling him and his boy's dope for years now. Through out that time Green Eyes had been straight up.

Jinger came back to the table smiling. Ezel threw his arm around her as she snuggled up under him.

"You good baby?"

"Yeah, I'm good."

"What O boy talking about?" Sony didn't have to say it, Ezel knew how curious he was to know. That's why he asked her with him right there.

"Who Green Eyes? He wanted to know did I have any girlfriends to hook him up with."

"I wonna know everything he said," Ezel said sternly looking at her. She looked at him curious wondering was he serious. Realizing he was a lump formed in her throat. She tried swallowing, but it wasn't going anywhere. It was a sign of fear. She began repeating their conversation. Ezel wanted to appease Sony. He always had Ezel's back, so Ezel wanted to let him know that there was nothing to worry about. After trying to repeat their conversation verbatim Ezel pulled her close whispering in her ear. "You wouldn't lie to me would you?"

"I wouldn't lie to you Ezel," she responded in her sweet innocent voice.

"Good, I'ma hold you to that."

****

"I don't know when the last time I brung a female that wasn't ma family here," Ezel said parking the Bentley.

He had a nice big house in Norristown PA. As he pulled up to it Jinger felt like she accomplished her goal something she rarely if ever did. The mission was to find where he lived and anything else she could. All of sudden things begin feeling anticlimactic. It was getting too good to end so soon. She knew if she told P-Hall where he lived they would probably kill him. Her free ride and thousand dollars a week will end. It wouldn't be anymore shopping sprees. Not in the exact words, but Ezel basically told her she was wifey. She knew if she kept playing her part that things were only going to get better.

The sound of crickets was the only noise Jinger heard when she got out of the car. Mentally she compared the neighborhood to Naysia's. His house was bigger and better though.

"You like it," he asked after letting her in? He closed the door pressing the code to the alarm. "I ain't going to lie I be getting lonely in here by myself. That's why a lot of times I don't even come home."

Yeah right, Jinger thought. She knew his lifestyle was far from lonely. While looking around she knew it was no way she was going to tell P-Hall. Only a fool would pass up on the opportunity that was present in front of her. Ezel was her first real baller, she refuse to mess that up. Catching a baller that really had it was almost every female in the hood dream. She felt like she succeeded. She thought about how proud her friends would be for her, especially if she came through in that Bentley. The thought made her smirk. *Things could only get better. I have to bring my girls in.*

"You choose to be lonely."

"That's true, but only because I can't trust everyone. Now that I have you I'm hoping I won't be so lonely."

Jinger didn't know what to say, she just blushed. Everything in her mind was scrambling.

"I'm offering my house to you. I'm saying, that's if you feel comfortable enough with me."

Jinger was slow to answer. She wanted to bad, but how could she? P-Hall would know she knew where he lived. That would mess everything up. Her mind raced in search of an answer until she found one.

"I'm comfortable with you, I just don't want to rush things. Let's take our time and see how things go."

"I respect that."

Jinger had put her innocent front on and again it worked like a charm. Playing this part was teaching her something she never knew. All this time she'd been giving herself to dudes freely thinking that would make them like her and in return she would be able to get love among other things out of them. That mentality was something she learned after going through her puppy love stages. She found out the hard way that boys didn't like being with one girl. She found herself in constant competition over boys, even fighting over them. Years later she started hanging with her current friends who are all older than her. They were having so much fun going out, messing with different dudes that she wasn't worried about being in a serious relationship.

Now that she thinks about it before she was way too young for a serious relationship. She watched her friends go in and out of relationships, dealing with dudes in the streets and it seemed that the only thing that determined if they were feeling a dude or not was money and status. Not if he was a good person or not. She eventually got on it like them. They only messed with street dudes. While some had more money than others none of the ones she dealt with had the kind of money Ezel had.

CHAPTER 15

JINGER WOULD STAY OVER EZEL'S HOUSE A COUPLE TIMES A week, reporting back to P-Hall as if she didn't know where he lived yet. Telling him that they stayed in this and that hotel, which was half true. She told him about certain clubs Ezel and his boys frequented. The dudes he be with, but never anything that P-Hall could trap Ezel off with. It didn't occur to P-Hall that she was holding back. Baby-K had told him that it wasn't going to be easy. Still he didn't feel how things were dragging out, so he followed Baby-K advice and asked Jinger to body Ezel herself.

They were in the kitchen standing by the sink. Jinger's eyebrows were raised in shock, her neck forced slightly back. She didn't know what P-Hall thought of her, but she wasn't about to kill anybody. She couldn't imagine an amount he could bribe her with, even if he could make her rich. It was no use of being rich in prison. That would hurt more than being broke she thought.

"That's too much P-Hall, I can't bring myself to do something like that."

P-Hall got the answer he expected, but desperate times call for desperate measures. He tried that's all he chalked it up to. He wanted badly to get rid of Ezel. He was trying harder than Baby-K. Baby-K would tell him the dudes he had on the job, how they were hunting him down. None of it seem to have anything on what he was doing. Seeing how arrogant Ezel was that day when they tried to talk to him really made P-Hall want his head.

"Alright, forget I asked that. I need the drop on this dude. Do he be coming to pick you up from Cortina's house?"

"Yeah but" …..

"Let me know next time so I can have ma men ready."

"If I do that he might suspect I had something to do with it."

"No he not."

Jinger could tell P-Hall was growing impatient. She was trying to give him what she could without messing up her thing. Ezel had been taking care of her, giving her money to go shopping. She coming back with Supreme, Prada, Gucci etc....She knew P-Hall wasn't going to take care of her. He wasn't her man, he's her aunt's man. Now when she went shopping she didn't have to steal. One of the best feelings in the world for her was shopping without having to look at the price tags. That was a feeling every woman wish they could have. On top of that she didn't have to worry about a security guard trying to arrest her.

One thing Jinger did tell P-Hall in that conversation was when and where the next time she was going to see Ezel at. P-Hall had to make a judgment call, he had to catch him where he could. From what she told him the laundry mat was the only place he knew for certain where he'll be.

****

Jinger had no idea that she was being watched as she pulled in front of the laundry mat. It was a regular Tuesday afternoon, every store on the street was busy. There was no shortage of cars going up and down the street. At the corner sat a black Malibu. Two dudes sat low in it watching the laundry mat. They weren't watching it for Jinger, but to see what dude she was going to be talking to. They didn't know what Ezel looked like. P-Hall gave them a brief description Since arriving they hadn't seen anyone who matched that description.

Once Jinger went in they got out of their car heading to the laundry mat stopping at the store right before it. Sneaking a peek through the laundry mat's big windows. It was daytime but they didn't care who saw them. Not even the cops could stop their mission. When they saw Jinger head to the back they moved out, hands on their waist as they treaded pass the few ladies doing laundry as their kids played together. The ladies knew something was about to happen. They quickly gathered their kids to get out of there.

Jinger hadn't been in the office two minutes before the door came crashing in, guns blazing. Ezel grabbed Jinger to the floor. She automatically screamed. He grabbed her close to him in an attempt to shield himself from the bullets. It kind of looked like he was trying to save her. They were on the floor behind the desk, he pulled out his 45. and began firing back. The two dudes didn't make it too far in the office. Ezel shot back rapidly emptying his clip then grabbed the shot gun that was hooked on to the bottom of the desk. Jinger was balled up with her head covered. Just when he cocked the shotty he heard their guns clicking and then footsteps running in the opposite direction.

"Hold up, I'm just getting started mothafuckas," he said getting up running after them. Bout time he got up and ran out front they were gone. He scanned the street seeing if any cars looked suspicious, then it occurred to him that he was standing outside of his business with a big shot gun in hand looking like a mad man. He tried to quickly make his way back inside. While doing so he felt a burning sensation in his leg that caused him to hobble a bit. When he looked down his pants leg was bloody. He got Jinger and they got out of there.

****

In the mid afternoon Ezel held on to Jinger as she knocked on his aunt's door. He secretly hoped, prayed, and wished that she was there so she could attend to his womb. Everything was answered when she opened the door.

"O my goodness baby, what's wrong," she asked letting them in.

"I got shot Auntie, I need help."

"Why didn't you go to the hospital?"

"I can't, they might lock me up?"

Knowing that her nephew was in the streets she didn't ask anymore questions. She went to get her medical kit.

"Bring him to the kitchen darling," she told Jinger.

Ezel sat on the kitchen floor, one leg out of his pants while his aunt attended to him.

"It don't look too bad, do it hurt?"

"Definitely."

"Well, the most I can do for you right now is wrap it up to stop the bleeding. Eventually you're going to have to go to the hospital so it won't get infected. You don't want to mess around and lose your leg."

Ezel's aunt had been in the medical field for almost twenty-five years. First being an LPN then becoming a nurse. She seen how bad an untreated womb could get.

When Ezel heard he could lose his leg he realized how serious it really was. He no longer wanted to delay going to the hospital.

"If you don't want to go to the one over here then go to the one in Camden, but no matter which one you go to they're going to report it. They have to. Just tell them anything, guys do It all the time. Do you want me to go with you?"

"Nah Auntie, I'm good. I'm going to take your advice and go to the one in Camden," Ezel said after she had cleaned his leg up.

"Be careful," his aunt said giving him a hug on his way out the door.

Jinger didn't have time to think, she was too busy running around with Ezel trying to get him taking care of. The hospital was the first moment she had got to herself. She was still in a state of shock. She wanted to go home just to get away from it all. She couldn't though, she had to be there for Ezel. He had taken a bullet to save her. She felt obligated to be by his side like any real chick should be, right? She asked herself mentally?

****

At Ezel's house Jinger sat in bed while Ezel slept. His womb was minor, but the medicine the hospital gave him had put him down. Jinger couldn't sleep. Even though Ezel had offered her to live with him and she had things over there, it wasn't home. Not even Naysia's house could provide her with the comfort she needed right now. She wanted to run home to her mommy where she felt the safest. Things had gotten real way too fast. They could have been killed. Reality was setting in, that she was dealing with a dangerous dude who was really involved in some shit. Her aunt had warned her. Remembering the look in his eyes when he was busting that gun like a mad man, not scared at all. Then how he got up and ran after them. What kind of lunatic would do something like that? She shook her head at the thought. Feel safe or scared, her feelings were confused. Especially since she was sent to cross him. That look told her that he's not the type of guy that'll take something like that lightly.

He saved me, he must really care about me. Forget that, the only reason you're here is to set him up. Wait, set him up, and mess up a good thing? How many chicks could say they found a dude that really got it and that really cared about them?

Not many she knew. She thought about all the men she knew who had money and nice things that treated females they were dealing with like crap. Even when the women weren't with them for their material things. She sat there struggling with her thoughts. Just when she thought she had made all the right moves that would make her life easier here go all this b.s.

****

The next morning Ezel woke up body aching and head throbbing. He held his head while squinting his eyes, "Ah shit," he murmured. For a minute he almost forgot about his leg until he tried to get up putting pressure on it. "Ah."

"Be careful," Jinger said.

Ezel didn't pay her any mind, he sat on the edge of the bed collecting his thoughts for a few seconds, then grabbed his phone. Thirty-seven missed messages and calls. The whole night dudes were trying to get in touch with him. Jinger talked to Sony while Ezel was in the hospital. She told him what had happened and that he was good. All the rest of the calls she didn't bother with. She wasn't about to be up all night answering his phone like some kind of secretary. Through his aunt his family found out what happened, so they were calling too.

Ezel's first call was to Sony, afterwards he laid back down.

"Go get me some ice water," he told Jinger.

"Are you hungry," she asked while getting up?

"Not right now."

"How you feeling?"

"Like shit," he said before taking a few gulps of his water. After burping he handed it off then laid back down.

Jinger sat the cup on the nightstand. She had only gotten about four hours of sleep herself but was still wide awake.

"You alright, I know yesterday wasn't something you looked forward to experiencing. Neither did I, but you know shit happens."

"I'm alright, thanks for pulling me out of the way."

On the inside Ezel was smiling. Little did she know that that wasn't his intentions for him pulling her down, but he'll definitely take the credit.

"That's what I'm supposed to do. I'll be crushed if anything was to happen to you." It was some truth to what he was saying only because he really liked her, but in moments like that when it's either him or her he'll prefer she take the bullets before him any day. He could get another chick, but he can't get another life.

Jinger brought every word he said. Him being crushed if anything was to happen to her showed her that he cared. A man expressing his feeling to her was something new, what more could a man do to prove that he'll do anything for a lady? Feeling safe and secure in his words she snuggled up to him as they laid there.

"You see now why I need someone I can trust? It's messed up to say, but I got an army full of dudes that'll do almost whatever I tell them. At the end of the day I can't trust any of them, only to a certain extent. The stuff I be having these dudes doing I don't want to trust them with all of that. It's about getting things done though. Every time it's a 50/50 chance they might get me for some money or drugs. Mostly all of them play the murder game, can't be around them too long outside a social setting. They might get some bright ideals. On top of that I got beef coming from all angle. You saw yesterday how real it is. Dudes coming for ma head. Everybody wants ma spot, everybody want the top, but they don't know that they can't handle it. This aint the corporate world, it's the streets. Never mind me, I'm venting. I got a lot on ma mind right now."

"It's okay, you can talk to me."

Ezel looked at her and nodded his head. He wrapped his arm around her bringing her closer. He kissed her forehead and said, "It's good to know I got ya ear when I need it."

Jinger never heard a hood dude vent before. From the outside looking in the streets seemed like a glorious life, especially his. He had everything a hood dude desired. She knew dudes be getting killed, but she thought it be random stupid petty stuff. Like most chicks she really didn't know the politics behind the killings. She just knew what the streets gossiped about. Now she was getting a feel for how real things were.

In a way Jinger was empathic, she remembered how stressed she was when she found out that dudes was trying to get at her. She fled the city she was so scared. Him on the other hand was some how able to function knowing he could be a victim any day.

Later that day Sony came over, he was the only one allowed to visit. Nobody else had that privilege. Out of respect Jinger went upstairs. That didn't stop her from ease dropping though.

****

"Ya boys aint get the job done," Baby-k told P-Hall.

"Yeah, I know," P-Hall responded sounding disappointed.

"That shit all on the news, talking about they're questioning the owner of the store. I know it aint him, he don't have shit in his name."

P-Hall nodded his head in agreement. "They said they're going to stay on his heels. They know they not getting the other half until he done up."

"Fuck it, we just going to keep sending dudes at him. Put out the S.O.S, broad day, wherever. We got an army full of blood thirsty goons, make them work."

P-Hall seen the agitation in Baby-K's face. The beef was not only messing with his money, but he couldn't move how he wanted without looking over his shoulders worrying about who trying to knock his head off. It's hard to relax when you know its people trying to kill you and you don't know what they look like.

"What's up with the little chick you had on the job?"

"I aint see her since that shit happened."

"You think she was there when it went down?"

"That's how I knew for sure he was going to be there. I Just hope she not bright enough to figure out I'm the one who sent them."

Baby-K nodded his head in agreement knowing that could mess things up. "She probably still with him then."

"If so he probably took her to his spot. Once we find out where he rest his neck its ball game."

"If he took her to his spot," Baby-K stated thinking Ezel wasn't that stupid.

CHAPTER 16

Naysia grew more and more worried about Jinger. She had been calling her ever since last night after Brandy told her that it was a shooting at Ezel's laundry mat. Brandy didn't know anything about Jinger. The news said that a man and a woman was seen leaving the scene. Naysia had an ideal who that woman was.

Later that night Jinger came home. When Naysia heard her pull up she got out of bed to look out the window. Bout time Jinger got in the house Naysia was downstairs comforting her.

"You don't know how to answer ya phone? You got me all worried about you. What happened?" Naysia bombarded her with questions.

"Aint no need to worry, I'm good."

"You could have at least called me back so I could know you was alright."

"You right, but I was busy. It was all kinds of stuff going on."

"I told you the type of person you're dealing with."

Jinger thought Naysia was overreacting, but Naysia was only trying to look out for her niece. One of her close friends had been killed while chilling with a dude she was messing with. She knew that just because Jinger was a female that didn't mean dudes wasn't going to get her if she was there.

While trying to relax in her room Jinger received a call from Ezel.

"Where you at? I want you here with me," he said before she could answer his question.

Jinger hesitated, she didn't want to stay with him, but was scared to deny him. "I'm home," she responded."

"I'm sending somebody to get you."

"No, here I come," she quickly said.

"You sure?"

"Yeah, I'm on my way."

Jinger seen that it was no way out of that one. If he would have sent someone to Cortina's house and she wasn't there after telling him she was she'll have some explaining to do. She left the house without Naysia knowing.

****

"I was missing you," Ezel said opening the door for her. His leg injury didn't allow him to move around how he wanted. Lately he had been playing the crib making his moves from there.

By the hug he gave her she could tell he was sincere about missing her. She never had someone be so sensual with her. The thought of setting him up was messing with her. The more time they spent together the fonder her heart became of him. Not falling for him became a struggle because of the circumstances. That was just one struggle, the other was trying to throw P-Hall off because she wasn't quite sure she wanted to go through with it anymore.

"I want you to stay with me tonight. I need you more than ever right now. I can't trust too many people."

"I'm here aint I," Jinger said grabbing the remote off the table.

"Yeah, but I don't understand. I offer you to come live with me and you decline. You rather stay in the city. I could have almost any chick out there. You see how hard they be trying to get ma attention when we out. They'll do whatever for the opportunity to come live with me."

"We'll get one of them then," Jinger acted like she was joking, but she really didn't like how he was throwing that in her face. They had developed their own little playful banter how couples usually do.

"If I wanted one of them I would have called them. I called you though, you special to me. You got this light to you, I can't explain it, but you do."

They sat on the couch, Jinger stared through the windows of his soul to see how serious he was. A light, that was the first time she had ever heard that corny line and she heard quite a few. Mainly from old heads trying to push up.

Ezel was referring to the good nature he thought he saw in her. Her potential, the feeling he got when he was around her, her smile, everything about her. She was always in a good mood. Her eyes still had life in them. She wasn't jaded like other chicks he knew.

"Tomorrow I want you to go shopping so you could have some things here. Get you some nice things too, don't worry about the prices."

The light he said he seen was shinning brighter than ever once she heard that. Jinger had her mind set on getting her weekly pay from P-Hall but decided that could wait. She knew Ezel was going to give her more than that to go shopping with.

Ezel not only gave her more than a stack, he let her push the Bentley too. Jinger called her girls to let them know that she was coming through. They had no idea she was going to come through how she did.

****

"Dam girl, you really doing the dam thing," Trudy said getting in the passenger seat.

"Yeah right," Shay said admiring the interior from the back seat. "I thought you had dudes over there to hook us up with."

When Jinger first told them she was plugging into some real dudes with money over there they didn't think too much of it, but seeing the Bentley was proof. They really wanted in now.

"I do Shay, trust me, I aint forget you."

The last person Jinger picked up was Stacy. Laquanda was left out, because of her kids she always had to find a babysitter. Jinger didn't want to ride five deep anyway, plus secretly she didn't feel comfortable around her because everyone was saying that she set her brother up. Since then everything has been awkward between them.

Before going shopping they cruise the streets of Camden. Jinger wanted everyone to see her pushing the Bentley. She wanted to have people talking about her, dudes and females. She didn't care if dudes who were trying to get at her heard that she was in the city. They stopped by Chase Street to buy some weed. Dudes was out there deep. A few tried to push up. Jinger took one guy number just because she didn't want to be ignorant. She knew if she was to act stuck up while driving a Bentley that they would probably trash it and start playing her out. She seen the funniest things happen to females who thought they were the shit. Plus, that wasn't her.

The whole ride all Shay and Stacy wanted to know was who were the dudes Jinger was going to plug them in with. What did they look like, and what kind of car did they drive? By the kind of car they drove that's how they were going to determine their worth. They were putting pressure on Jinger. The only one that wasn't saying anything was Trudy. Jinger knew exactly who she was going to plug in with whom. She gave them brief descriptions and told them enough about the men to try to shut them up, but that only made them want to know more.

****

P-Hall was disappointed when Jinger wasn't at Naysia's house. She wasn't answering her phone either. He felt as though she was losing focus. Usually she'll beat him there to get paid. A thousand dollars was a lot of money for most people. The only people that didn't show up for that kind of money were people who could afford not to. In that case if she could afford not to that meant Ezel must be treating her real well, which for P-Hall wasn't a good thing.

"She was here last night. I don't know when she left. I told her about answering her phone. Do you know she was in that shooting that happened at some laundry mat that Ezel own?"

P-Hall seen the concern on Naysia's face. He didn't share the same sentiments, all he wanted to know was where she was at, and what info could she give him.

"This girl stressing me out, I'm not feeling good. I was throwing up earlier."

"You should go get checked out," P-Hall suggested.

Naysia had a feeling why she was feeling how she was feeling but wanted to make sure. Not only did she want to make sure, but she had to decide if she was going to keep it or not. In the back of her mind she knew she had sex with Steve without a condom and that it was a slight chance that if she was pregnant it could be his. Even though it was only once she had to decide if she wanted to roll the dice.

"You that sick?"

Naysia shook her head, yeah.

"Alright, don't worry about it, I'll have somebody else do it. Tell Jinger I need to see her. Tell her to call me a-sap," he said before leaving.

Naysia thought her being sick would want P-Hall to spend some time with her, take care of her to make sure she was good. He had other things to do though. Things he considered more important than making sure she was alright. His insensitivity had her thinking about how caring Steve was. In every aspect they were like night and day.

How P-Hall would take her being pregnant crossed her mind. They been dealing with each other for six years and the only time she get pregnant is after she slept with another man. That's the main reason she suspected it might be Steve's. She didn't know if P-Hall could have kids, he didn't have any with his girl either.

****

Later that night Jinger showed up at Naysia's house. Ezel would have let her use the Bentley all-day, but she took it back before going there.

"P-Hall said call him," Naysia said.

Jinger looked at her in the bed, how she was all wrapped up with the bucket next to the bed. "What's wrong," she asked?

"I'm pregnant," she said reaching on the nightstand showing Jinger the pregnancy test. "Don't tell P-Hall, I go to the doctors tomorrow to make sure."

"That's good news," Jinger said trying to cheer her up. She had no idea about her aunt's dilemma. When she called P-Hall he was already on his way to the house.

＊＊＊＊

"Come here yo, talk to me, ya aunt told me about what happened. You alright," P-Hall asked acting concerned?

They sat on the couch and he tried to get it all out of her. Still she gave him as little as possible. Nothing about Ezel's aunt house or that she was staying with him.

"So where did ya'll go?"

"To the Ritz Carlton."

P-Hall could sense that she wasn't being truthful. He could feel it, he still paid her for her useless services. It was then that he knew he had lost her. He sat there looking at the lies come out of her face undecided if he was going to call things off or not. He knew if Ezel had her he had her. That was the only thing about sending females to handle things like this. Dick and material things were always going to be their weakness.

"I do remember him and his boy Sony talking about getting at somebody name Baby-K. They said he had something to do with the shooting at the laundry mat."

"What did they say about him?"

"They know where his kids go to school at." Jinger divulged that information because she didn't want whatever was going to happen to them kids on her conscious.

Finally, her worthless ass is good for something, P-Hall thought. He didn't tell her Baby-K was his manz. He acted as if that info was useless too, but as soon as he got the chance he called Baby-K.

＊＊＊＊

The next day Baby-K had his lady called the school to let them know that his kids wouldn't be coming in today. He wasn't going to risk some fools trying to kidnap his kids. Never had he been a gambler and he wasn't about to start. The beef he was in wasn't a game. What really had him puzzled was how did they know where his kids went to school? The other question was did they know where he live? Four goons patrolled the school facility in a black Chrysler van. Only the two front windows weren't tinted up. For that reason only the driver sat up front. They slow rolled down the street looking for anything suspicious or out of the ordinary.

"You see that," Chew asked looking through the back tint? The other two adjusted themselves for a view.

"Yeah," one responded.

"They aint sitting there for nothing, their elementary days been up," Chew said cocking the AK. "Go back around. Its show time boys."

No matter how much chew talked his tooth pick never left his mouth. Only when he was about to put in work did he chew one, hence the name chew. Only Baby-K and P-Hall knew that was the reason that had became his attribute. None of their other dudes went back that far with them. The only other person who knew him like that was Ezel.

Kids were still flocking to school in packs. Some stopped at a nearby corner store, while a crossing guard helped others across the street. None of them had any ideal that they were about to witness their first murder. A moment in their lives that they'll never forget. Depending on how much of it they were exposed to some will have nightmares, while some will be traumatized, and for some it won't affect them at all. They'll act like it wasn't their first time seeing such an act, and it probably wasn't. For the rest of their lives they'll talk about the times they witnessed this and that person getting killed. More than likely they'll be the ones to get involved in the streets.

Nobody could tell Chew that he wasn't in the military, them was his favorite flicks. As the van slowly approached the car he barked his last commands before pulling his mask over his face. The van sped up then stopped on a dime. The door slid open and the choppers rang off. Kids were running, screaming, and yelling. Almost every car alarm in the area went off as the shots echoed for blocks and blocks. The van tires screeched as they zoomed off leaving the three men in the car a bloody mess.

****

"Yeah, I already know, I'll meet you at the spot tonight." Ezel ended his call and flung his phone on the couch.

Seeing that he wasn't in a good mood Jinger got up about to go up stairs to give him his space.

"Come here," he told her.

She had no idea that she was the cause of three dudes being murdered. All she knew was that he was furious about something. She stood in front of him with his hair frizzed up and his eyes redder than normal and wondered what was bothering him so much.

"We going out tonight baby, but I want you to meet me there. I got a few things I have to handle first. You know the spot I took you before, right?"

"Umm hmm, can I bring my girlfriends?"

"Yeah, bring whoever," he said not giving it any thought. He was just trying to get out to clear his mind. "I'ma need you to pick something up from the laundry mat for me tomorrow."

"The laundry mat," Jinger asked worried?

"Yeah, don't worry, you good. Don't nobody know you. That's why I'ma need you to start picking ma money up on the regular. Look, you have to understand that I'm putting a lot of trust in you. This aint no little money I'ma be having you pick up. I take this shit serious. You ma lady, but you fuck up and cross me I'ma treat you accordingly. I got faith in you though. I'll explain everything to you tomorrow, just meet me at the spot tonight."

He kissed Jinger on the forehead before leaving. The threat didn't register until he left. He said it so smooth she questioned was it really a threat. A threat was supposed to make one feel scared, she wasn't scared at all. The fact that he was going to trust her with his money made her feel secure, even important. It meant so many things that the threat flew right over her head. At that point there was no turning back. No matter how much she tried to play him from a distance it didn't work. Now she wanted to show him she was down for him. In his profession that's what dudes be wanting. The more love he showed her and trusted her, the more she fell in love with him. All she ever wanted was a man to love, cherish, and have faith in her, and put her in a position to thrive. She couldn't tell him how much it meant to her, but she planned on showing him.

****

Ezel and Sony sat in the VIP section talking. The Music wasn't that loud back there as it was through out the rest of the club so they were able to hear each other clearly. This was the family club, mostly everyone in there had some type of affiliation with them. If anyone came in there with any drama they must have a death wish.

"Shit like that just don't happen, he had to have known." Ezel was convinced that that was the only explanation.

"I see what you saying, I been trying to figure out how he knew though. The chick said he take his kids to school everyday no matter what."

"If she the only one that knew she might of did some bullshit. What you think?"

"I don't think so, if it was like that she could have just not told me."

Sony knew where Ezel was going with it, but he wasn't thinking the same. He happen to be smashing a chick that use to mess with Baby-K. She the one who told him that Ezel always took his kids to school. It was the reason when she did stay with Baby-K that he would have to leave before the sun came up.

"Alright man, if you say so. Jinger going to be doing money pick ups for me from now on."

"You trust her like that?"

"I gotta trust somebody, right? I warned her not to cross me. I want you to send somebody too. If you don't trust them like that then follow them, but I don't want you showing ya face there. Dudes might try to slide on you next."

Jinger and her friends got let in free of charge. By now most of Ezel's comrades knew who Jinger was. As she led the pack to their table dudes kept asking about her friends. Shay, Trudy, and Stacy were looking exceptional in tight dresses that hugged their tight bodies. Mostly every guy in there was ogle eyeing them. There was a table reserved for them with a bottle of Rose on ice.

"You really out here having it," Trudy said as they sat. She was impressed. "Look at her," she said now referring to Shay.

"Look at me what," Shay said grabbing the bottle. She had been smiling hard. All the attention had her open. Jinger had told them not to pay them other guys any mind, that she had dudes she was going introduce them to. One dude had came over trying to be extra friendly with Jinger, she let him know that they were waiting for Ezel and Sony. That quickly got rid of him.

"Who was that," Shay asked once he left?"

"His name Tim, that's not who I want you to meet. He was on ya'll though. He wouldn't ever have come over here if Ezel was over here. Shay don't drink so much, told you I'm over here playing innocent. That means ya'll can't be acting up. Aint nothing slow about these dudes."

"Look who's talking about messing something up, every time we get into something it's because of you. I got this sis, I could handle myself," Shay said as the suds overflowed on her glass. She hurried the glass to her lips before she made a mess.

Jinger exhaled pouting her lips with her eyebrows raised looking at Trudy and Stacy like it was going to be a long night. They sat there talking, laughing, and enjoying themselves. Occasionally people were stopping by speaking to Jinger, some females but mainly guys trying to push up on her friends.

Jinger didn't know that Ezel was already there. She was expecting him to pop up at any moment. Instead him and Sony talked and watched her and her friends from the VIP section.

When Green Eyes showed up Shay was in the bathroom. He sat next to Jinger and began chatting the ladies up. Stacy and Trudy knew who he was from the description Jinger gave of him. Shay didn't have any clue who he was when she came back from the bathroom. "Green Eyes this ma friend Shay, Shay this is Green Eyes." She had already introduced him to the others.

"Come on cutie, it's enough room for you right here," he said patting the seat next to him for shay to sit.

He look good, good looking Jinger, Shay thought to herself as she sat next to him. Green Eyes immediately zoned in on Shay while still entertaining the whole table. One time he said something that had the whole table cracking up. While they were laughing, he placed his hand on Jinger's thigh under the table. Nobody could see it. Jinger tensed up but didn't say anything. She was uncomfortable. While laughing he looked at her and winked his eye then removed his hand. She was relieved when he removed it. She hoped he wouldn't do anything like that again.

He gotta know better, he must be taking my friendliness for something else, Jinger thought. Messing with one of Ezel's friends was something that she was not willing to do no matter how good he looked. She had it way too good. More than ever she was convinced that she wasn't going to mess up what she had going on for anybody.

****

"I wonder what's so funny," Sony said as him and Ezel watched Green Eyes entertain the ladies.

"You hard on him, lighten up a little. You know how he is. He probably down there trying to laugh his way into one of Jinger's friends' panties."

Ezel tried to bring a positive outlook to the situation, but when he looked at Sony he was serious still looking at them. Sony's vibe was always serious, but Ezel could sense something else.

"What's up with you and Green Eyes? I get the feeling you don't dig him. Every time he around ya'll don't really say much to each other."

"I'm saying that's ya manz, so I keep it fly with him. I just don't like the loud slick talking shit. Dudes like that are always suspect to me, like they always up to something. It's hard for me to trust them type."

"You gotta give people a chance sometimes. Come on, I know you see one of Jinger friends you wonna get at." Ezel threw his arm around Sony and led him to Jinger's table.

Shay was already tangled in Green Eyes web. Every word he said she hung on to, laughing too hard at things that weren't that funny. When Ezel and Sony went over there the attention shifted from Green Eyes to them. Jinger introduced Ezel and Sony to her Friends. Afterwards she fell back while they all got to know one another. Jinger's friends couldn't but be themselves. She just hoped that they didn't blow it. She brung them in, everything else was up to them.

CHAPTER 17

Jinger pulled up in front of the laundry mat, got out, and then took two bags from the back seat. While going in she noticed that the windows that were shot out during the shooting were fixed. *That was fast,* she thought as she went inside. Once inside she noticed everything was back to normal. She put the bags in a cart and pushed it to the machine closest to Ezel's office. After putting a load in she sat on the bench looking around. All she knew was the code word and that she was to meet a woman. All the people in there were women. About a good ten minutes rolled by before a lady in her late forties who had already been in there came over with her cart and got on the machine next to hers. Jinger played like she was active on her phone but she was aware of the lady's every move.

"Can I use your phone," the lady asked?"

They were the words she had been waiting for. She looked up at her, the lady smirked knowing she didn't really want to use Jinger's phone.

"It's in them two bags in the cart," the lady told Jinger.

"Thank you," Jinger said returning her smile.

Before doing anything Jinger observed her surroundings. Once she seen everyone was in their own little world she got up and left with the two bags. The lady sat there watching the clothes Jinger had left in the machine as if they were hers.

Jinger could no longer fight the urge to take a peek in the bags. She pulled over and grabbed one of the bags from the back seat. Ezel told her that it was money but seeing it left her mouth gaping. Never had she seen so much money before. She closed it back up not seeing what they had to be so discreet about. In her naïve mind it was only money, who gets in trouble for having money?

Ezel was more than glad to see her when she came through the door with the bags. She had proven herself trustworthy, and reliable. He kissed her on the forehead, took the bags then headed to the table so he could recount everything himself. In the lifestyle he lived one could never be too cautious.

****

Shay woke up with a hangover grabbing her head as she sat up. She looked over at Green Eyes still sound asleep. That's when everything came back to her about what Jinger had told them. She did exactly what Jinger told them not to do, have sex on the first night. Still she didn't have any regrets. She could honestly say she tried her hardest to hold out, but every kiss he planted on her made her wetter and wetter. He was all over her squeezing and grabbing her butt, pressing his hard on against her, kissing her face and neck. The whole time she was trying to tell him that she wasn't that type of girl, but her body language said she wanted him. Everything he did to her she enjoyed and wanted him to do more of. Before she knew it she was moaning as he kissed all her hot spots. When he got to the pussy he found that thing dripping wet. She squirmed and moaned as he licked her juices.

The sex was all she could hope for and better. From the way he was laying there she could tell it was good for him too. Only thing she was hoping was that he didn't see her as a jump off because she let him hit so fast. Even though she didn't have any regrets she still couldn't help to feel that she had messed things up as far as enjoying the benefits of having a dude with money. From experience whenever she had a one night stand the dudes never took her serious, or even called her again unless they wanted some more pussy.

"You alright," she heard a voice say.

She turned back at Green Eyes smiling.

"Come here, lay with me."

They both were still naked under the covers. Shay laid back down and he wrapped his arms around her.

"I really like you. We going to have to do this more often," he said grinning.

"Green Eyes, I don't want you to think I'm some kind of hoe. I enjoyed last night, but…."

"Even the sex," he asked cutting her off?

Shay smiled. "Even the sex, but we're going to have to get to know one another with the intentions of building a relationship." She thought about how those words didn't even sound right coming out of her own mouth, which caused her to wonder how it sounded to him.

Green Eyes had heard that same spiel more times than he could count. He knew all he had to do was play along and he could hit whenever he wanted. "I'm cool with that. I don't think any less of you because of last night. In fact I want you even more."

Shay was a little amazed by his answer. She knew he was different, dudes from Camden were so ignorant she probably wouldn't have worked up the courage to say those things. Green Eyes was saying all the right things, she couldn't help but think he was a tender dick dude. She was feeling him though.

****

"I can't believe this shit," Naysia said entering the house. Her first pregnancy and she didn't know who the father was. She was madder at herself than anyone else. She slept with Steve out of spite. All because she assumed P-Hall and Jinger was creeping. Now she had to face the fact that there was a chance the baby could be Steve's. A small chance she told herself, yet a chance she had to take. She wasn't willing to have an abortion. Just knowing that she was pregnant meant there was a baby growing inside of her. She wasn't going to kill it.

CHAPTER 18

"Everything was there, right," Sony asked Ezel?

"Of course, why wouldn't it be, he answered?

"Just making sure, she pulled over and took a look in the bags."

Jinger didn't know that Sony had observed the whole transaction. Then followed her to Ezel's house. He wanted that money to really get to where it had to go. Since he wasn't making the drop off himself, the only way to make sure of that was to follow it. He was cautious like that.

"Yeah, I figure she might do something like that. It's nothing though. She probably wanted to see if it was really money in there or not. She didn't take anything that's all that matters. Did she look nervous?"

"She looked normal."

A little too normal, Sony thought to himself. He wasn't about to tell Ezel that because he seen how serious he was taking her and he was the one telling him that he should at least snatch up a chick to have kids with.

"There she go right there, almost done," Ezel said referring to the building as they approached the construction site. I'm trying to hurry these mothafuckas up, so I could have everything done by next month."

"You can't rush them if you want it done right."

"Man, you know how it is, the anticipation and all that."

Ezel had copped a store in a strip mall, it was getting renovated. He planned on turning it into a clothing store. Most of his ideas he ran by Sony to see what he thought. Sony was happy for his dude. He knew how enthusiastic he was about it. That's the kind of dude Sony was. Ezel had looked out for him so Sony was to forever be there for his manz.

"I know one thing you forgot. I haven't heard you mention it yet."

Ezel thought for a second, and then it dawned on him. "I know, you talking about the name. I'm still thinking about that."

"How you not have that on cap? The name is everything, that's part of ya promotion. You name it some goofy shit aint nobody going to be trying to come through."

"You right, this shit aint like the drug game when you know mothafuckas are going to come cop. I have to get on that. I think I'm a let Jinger run it. Put her and a couple of her bad friends in there, have dudes coming in chasing, fake balling. You know how dudes are, what you think?"

"You right, dudes see broads in there they going to spend that bread."

"What's up with Jinger's friend, you ever hit?"

"Nah, she was on me, but was trying to act like she don't be giving that thing up. I'm going to hit though."

The head construction worker came out. Him and Ezel began talking about the progress that was being made and what had to be finished. Ezel was involved in the development of the store. He stayed on the workers to make sure they finished everything on time and on budget.

****

"Where did he take you when ya'll left," Shay asked Stacy?

They were in Shay's house talking about their night out. Jinger wasn't there, but a few of their other friends were. Stacy was giving them the beat down [story] about how they came through with Jinger. The love and attention they were getting because they were with her, and the dudes they got introduced to. She was feeding them the fantasy, making it sound more glamorous than it was. While she told the story they envisioned every detail, all the way to the point when they left the building.

"He took me home."

"Home, he aint try to get any," Shay asked knowing how they usually did theirs? They were always game for a good time.

"No, I had let him know from the get-go that I wasn't that type of lady, so like a gentleman he took me home."

Some of her friends were laughing at the bullshit of her not being like that. The others were cutting their eyes because they didn't believe her.

"Ya'll bitches play too much. What ya'll laughing for?" Stacy asked smiling, she knew they were trying to clown her.

"We were laughing because you was dead serious when you said that."

"I had to be. You remember what Jinger said?"

"I know what she said but look," Shay said making a face twisting up her mouth. They all knew what that meant. "Green Eyes was looking way to good to be getting dropped off. I acted like I was trying to hold out, but that didn't last long."

"You a whore," Stacy joked.

"Thank you for the compliment. This whore threw it on him and I'ma see him again tonight, thank you," Shay said with conceit. She was proud of herself. A baller in the bag was something they all wish they had. She went on giving them a play by play of her night with Green Eyes.

CHAPTER 19

STACY KNEW THAT SHE WAS DEALING WITH A STREET DUDE, and how impatient they could be when it came to females giving them the booty. What one lady don't do the next one always will. She didn't know how long she should hold out. Jinger didn't tell her that part. She just knew that one of her closest friends had come up off of one of his friends, so her advice was worth taking. Never would she have thought that Jinger would come through in a Bentley. Her standards were so low she didn't think that was achievable. Now seeing that it was tangible motivated her. She was willing to be on her best behavior to secure that bag.

Sony picked Stacy up in his white on white Audi-s8. She came out wearing her best, a Gucci dress she stole a couple months ago. As she walked towards the car she checked herself out through the tinted windows. He knew what she was doing because he did it every time before he got in his car.

They went to a Kevin Hart comedy show over Philly. It was sold out, about sixty thousand came out to support the hometown comedian. Stacy had never been to any type of concert before. She didn't tell Sony that though. They laughed, ate, and drank, afterwards Stacy thought he was going to try to take her to the hotel to get some. She was used to things playing out like that. Dudes giving just to get. Still within she debated the whole idea. Rather to give in to him or drag things out a little longer. She was definitely attracted to him, even had plans on eventually giving him some. She just wanted things to be right so she could get what Jinger got, that life.

As they rode there was a moment of silence, she thought about how different Sony seemed. So well polished, quiet, and laid back, yet still hood. Even though that never really showed in his manner-isms. It was something she knew. She had seen him in his element a couple days ago at the club. Even then he was a perfect gentleman like she never saw before. *This must be what real bosses are like*, she thought to herself. That caused her to wonder other things like how old he was, when was his birthday etc…, things she didn't feel was appropriate to ask at the moment, yet that was all the questions he had been asking her. He knew a lot about her, but she knew nothing about him.

As he focused on the road she looked over at his perfect shape up. A Touch of Magic barbers was probably the best with them ra-zors. A dead man could get a date after one of them cuts. Sony had his left knee up near the door of the car while controlling the wheel at 9 O'clock. Stacy admired his style as they cruised the highway. He could feel her eyes caressing his face. He played it cool though. While turning off the exit he caught her staring and gave her a little smirk.

"What's up, you alright?"

"I'm okay," she responded blushing.

Sony nodded his head still smirking. A couple of blocks later he pulled in front of this park. Stacy looked at him, but he already had one foot out the door. "Come on."

Stacy took her time getting out. He was outside of her door wait-ing. He closed the door behind her then wrapped his arm around her and they began walking.

"Where are you taking me?"

"For a little walk."

"Sure you not trying to kidnap me," Stacy asked wrapping her arm around his waist as they walked.

"You can't kidnap the willing."

"You right."

"I aint kidnapping you, I wanted to go somewhere away from the noise so we could chill. I can't walk the streets where I'm from, that's one of the cons of the life I live. You know it's like anything else, you have to sacrifice something's for the things you really want.

Even though Stacy had no idea where they were she felt safe in Sony's arms. She didn't know it, but Sony was inclined to give her more respect than he would have any other woman who he had met in the club because she was Jinger's friend and Jinger was his manz girl.

****

Naysia had broken the news to P-Hall and was waiting for a response, but there was none.

"Did you hear me," she asked as he walked by her.

"Of course I heard you," he said with an attitude.

"Well," she stood there with her hands on her hips as he picked up his phone.

His mind was preoccupied with street stuff. Especially with Jinger, he hadn't seen her in weeks. She hadn't been picking up her phone. He know she seen his number. He could understand if she couldn't pick up right then and there, but not getting back to him that was a problem.

Naysia walked over to him and mushed him.

"Yo, what the fuck," he said as he jumped up and grabbed her by the neck driving her back towards the wall. The look on her face was one of shock. This was his first-time putting hands on her. He held her against the wall by the neck. She closed her eyes scared and in pain. Seeing her hurt made him realize what he was doing. He unhanded her immediately.

"I'm sorry baby," he said pulling her in. She wrapped her arms around him and wept. He felt bad for what he had done. "Naysia, you know I would never do anything to hurt you, I just got a lot on my mind baby."

He kissed her cheek and neck in an effort to calm her down and cheer her up. He held her tight letting her know in everyway he could that he loved her. After she stop crying they went over to the couch and sat down. He held her hand giving her his undivided attention.

Naysia wiped the remaining tears from her chin. "I was telling you that I'm pregnant, but you act like you don't care."

"I do care, that's good news. Come here." He brung her in for another hug and kiss.

"So you want me to keep it?"

"Of course, I'm Muslim. I'm not with that abortion stuff."

Naysia was glad to hear that because she also wanted to keep it.

"What about your girl?"

"Look, your having my baby she's not. I know what you thinking, don't worry. I'ma do the right thing, just give me some time."

P-Hall was saying everything he could to cheer her up. He didn't like seeing her like that. They had little disagreements before, never an argument. Those moments would usually end in them playing around. He didn't know what had just come over him, that's how he knew that the thing he was going through with Jinger was really messing with him.

"I don't want to do any of that other stuff for you either. I don't want to take them risk anymore."

"Alright, I can get other people to do it, it's nothing."

Through Naysia P-Hall would transport some of his dope and serve some of his weight drops. Now that she was pregnant she didn't want any parts of that. She knew that if he really cared about her he wouldn't allow her to do it anymore.

****

Days later P-Hall ran into Jinger on South Street outside of Platinum. She was with her friends. They were smiling, looking like they were enjoying themselves with shopping bags in their hands when he approached them.

"When were you going to get at me? I had been waiting."

Even though she acted like she wasn't Jinger was a little startled to see him there. "In due time, you worry too much. I got this."

Jinger had a little smirk on her face. P-Hall didn't find anything amusing or funny. He took what they had going on serious, but Jinger had the slightest idea of how serious things really were.

"I don't worry too much, you on some bullshit. You aint sticking to the fucking script."

P-Hall started speaking in an aggressive condescending tone while trying not to lose his cool. Jinger's friends were right there listening to everything wondering who he was and what is he talking about. "Ma peoples told me they saw you and ya friends in O boy Bentley. You think am stupid?"

One of P-Hall's manz had seen Ezel's Bentley thinking he had the drop on him. He squatted only to see a female in it. When he reported back to P-Hall, P-Hall had asked what she looked like and his manz described Jinger to a tee. Once he heard bright burgundy hair everything he thought became clear.

Jinger became embarrassed and started getting an attitude. Her friends being around only added pressure to the situation.

"I don't think you stupid" ….

"Yes the fuck you do. It's off. I aint paying you shit. You wasn't telling me nothing but useless shit anyway."

"So what, I don't need ya money anyway. I'm good," she said holding up her bags to let him know that she had her own money. She had a big grimy smile on her face that let him know he had got played. "Thanks for everything."

He knew she was talking about plugging her in with Ezel. That really hurt him because he basically helped her come up by doing that.

"I'll expose you."

"You don't want to do that because two can play that game."

P-Hall blood boiled as she turned her back to him and stepped off. All her friends had smirks on their faces like they were proud of the way their girl handled herself.

"Who was that," the ever so nosy Shay had to asked?"

"Some lame," Jinger said trying to keep her from asking any more questions.

****

Jinger had the Bentley parked on a lone street in front of a parking meter. Three cop cars were around it. One officer standing next to it was writing something on a pad.

"You must didn't put enough change in the meter," Trudy said."

"Why would they need three cops for that," Jinger wondered?

As they got closer they seen damages, windows busted out etc....

"Excuse me officer, this is my car, can you tell me what happened?"

While the officer was explaining that someone had shot the car up a tow truck was turning onto the street.

"We're going to have to impound it for investigation. You'll be able to come downtown to the police station in a couple days to retrieve it."

Jinger was furious, she cursed P-Hall, but more than anything she was worried that Ezel wouldn't let her use the Bentley again or trust her enough to give her any more privileges for that manner. She called him immediately using her sob voice. One of Ezel's dudes came to pick them up taking her friends to Camden then her to the site of Ezel's new store. He was there staying on top of things as usual.

Jinger got out of the passenger side with her five bags and sad face. She walked right into Ezel's arms.

"I don't know who did it, it was packed. When we came back it was all these cops around the car," she said sobbing.

"Don't worry about it, a car is just that, a car. As long as you good, I aint worried."

He kissed her forehead and told her to put her bags in the car. Referring to the red 760 BMW he was driving. As she did that he went and spoke a few words to his manz who had picked her up. They shook hands then dude pulled off. Jinger came back empty handed. Ezel took her a few stores down in front of his store.

"I'm about to turn this into a clothing and sneaker store, what you think?"

"It's big," she replied.

"Wait until you see the inside."

He took her in there telling her how he was going to set everything up, trying to give her his vision as he once did Sony. He had everything mapped out. This was his first time telling her anything about it. There were plenty of things she still didn't know about him.

"What do you think about running the laundry mat for me? That way you already be there when the money come. You don't have to do anything but open and close. It runs itself basically. Of course, once this opens you can run this if you want," he said referring to the clothing store.

Jinger was thinking about how she didn't want to run no laundry mat, but she didn't want to let him down. He was doing so much for her. She knew it had to come with a price. No matter the form it was in, wasn't nothing in the world free. That was something she was starting to realize. The one upside was that now that P-Hall was off her back she could deal with Ezel how she wanted to.

CHAPTER 20

"YOUR NIECE ALMOST MADE ME SLAP THE SHIT OUT OF HER," P-Hall told Naysia.

"Why you say that."

They were talking as they came out of the house and got into Naysia's Jaguar. P-Hall got in the driver seat.

"Nah, she think I'm stupid, I'm feeling like she was playing me the whole time. She out buying all this designer stuff. She wasn't going to go through with that shit. Then she had a nerve to tell me thanks for plugging her in with O' boy. You just don't know what I felt like doing to her. She knows way more than what she been telling me. Where she been staying at? Not here, because she been staying with him. I aint stupid. I really live this shit, she lucky she ya niece."

"Calm down, I'll talk to her," Naysia said rubbing the back of P-Hall's head while he drove.

They pulled over at the doctor's office. Naysia had a black and yellow and white sun dress on, some red bottoms, and a black Louis Vitton clutch purse in hand. This was Naysia second doctors visit, and she wanted P-Hall to be there all the way that's why she brung him.

The doctor asked Naysia multiple questions. She kindly answered all of them. The whole time P-hall sat next to her quiet. Once the doctor was done with the questions Naysia laid down for an ultrasound. For the first time they were able to see the life they had created on a monitor. She was only about eight weeks so it was only a little image on the screen, but that still caused Naysia to become emotional. P-Hall felt the same as he did when he first found out that she was pregnant.

"At this stage you're eight weeks. You should be due by March 14," the doctor said. He scheduled them for another routine checkup.

Gave them a copy of the ultrasound, and some other papers before they left.

"This is our first baby picture," Naysia said as they pulled off. The whole ride she kept looking at the ultrasound. P-Hall could feel her joy, he just wasn't used to the emotional stuff. He been let her know that he was happy that she was having his baby. What man doesn't want kids to carry his legacy?

While they drove P-Hall noticed a police car tailing him. He didn't say anything about it to Naysia. She was steady talking. Even though P-Hall didn't have any license he wasn't worried. All the paperwork on the car was legit. He figured the cop was just running the plates. He did a sly move strapping his seatbelt on. He drove proper, doing all the right things. The police still put the sirens on. The sirens caused Naysia to look up checking the side mirror. She had no idea they were being followed.

"Dickhead," P-Hall said to himself as he pulled over. "Be cool, I got this."

Naysia wasn't worried about if he had it or not. She was secretly praying that it wasn't Steve. It was no way for her to be cool with them thoughts.

It felt like Dejavu to Steve as he approached the Jaguar from the back. While following it he noticed that it wasn't Naysia, but a man who was driving. He tapped the window and P-Hall rowed it down.

"License and registration," Steve said looking in the car with the serious face. Naysia and his eyes connected, but Steve didn't skip a beat. Naysia sat there not saying anything. She didn't give him any funny looks or anything just had let him do his job. P-Hall dug in the glove department as Steve watched him intensely making sure paperwork was the only thing he was digging for.

"Here's my registration and insurance, I don't have a license."

Steve didn't say anything. He walked back to his car to run P-hall's name. After doing so he came back to the car and asked P-Hall to step out. He searched P-Hall then sat him on the curve. He got Naysia out of the car, but didn't search her, instead he began searching the car. He picked the ultrasound up off the seat, took it out and started looking at it. *This chick pregnant,* he thought to himself. He flung the ultrasound back on the passenger seat and called Naysia back to the car.

"Pregnant huh, do we need Murray to find out who the father is?" Naysia looked around nervous hoping P-Hall didn't hear that.

"I'm not going to blow your spot up, but I do want to know. You have to drive since ya drug dealer boyfriend don't have license," Steve said walking to P-Hall handing him two tickets. "Your girlfriend has to drive since she's the one with license. Ya'll can go."

Naysia felt like a weight was lifted when he left. He destroyed her moment. Her underarms had been perspiring and her panties were in a bunch. P-Hall didn't notice any of this. He was leaned back with his arm behind his head chilling as Naysia drove.

****

Ezel had got his sister to get his car out of the police impound lot since it was in her name. He took it back to the dealer so the parts could be replaced with official Bentley parts. When he got the call letting him know that it was ready him and Sony went to go pick it up.

"Look at my baby, all brand new." he said as they brung his car out. They want to be shooting a car. What ma car ever do to them, know what I'm saying? When ma shooters go in they aint aiming at cars they aiming at bodies. Aint no getting took to the dealership to get ya parts replaced. They gone to the morgue in body bags. Shit like that, feel me? I'm glad my little chick wasn't in there though." He said that thinking about how bad his car looked.

"How she holding up," Sony asked remembering Ezel told him how distraught she was when the incident first happened?

"She good, I know she think I'ma be on some bullshit with letting her push the wheels again. I aint on it like that though, this happened because of shit I got going on. She been going through it with me lately. First the shooting, then this car thing. I give it to her though, she thorough. She aint one of them complaining as broads."

The guy got out of the car and handed Ezel the keys. Ezel handed him a hundred-dollar tip. He pulled out of the dealership and Sony followed him in Ezel's BMW.

****

"Hello," Jinger answered.

"It's me, Naysia. Haven't heard from you in a few days now, I been worried.

"I'm good Aunt Naysia, I just been working."

"Working, you? I don't believe it, where?

"I'm running the laundry mat for Ezel. I don't really do anything."

Naysia was smiling on the other end of the phone. She knew that if her niece did have a job it didn't require her to do much of anything.

"After what happened you sure you want to work there?"

"Yeah, it's cool, everything fixed up and back to normal. It's business as usual," Jinger stated like the night she almost got shot was nothing.

"P-Hall told me that ya'll had a little argument."

"A little argument, did he tell you that he shot the car up I was driving?"

"Ya car?"

"No, Ezel's Bentley."

"He didn't tell me that." Naysia was disappointed that he would do something like that. "I can't have ya'll two beefing. I'ma need ya'll to peace things up."

"I don't have any problems with him, he mad at me."

"Alright, well come over when you get off so ya'll can have a heart to heart."

"I'll try to be there around dinner time."

"Alright, love you, bye."

"Love you too, bye bye."

The whole time Jinger was talking she was sitting in the back office watching the surveillance monitors. That was basically all she had to do, that and give people change for a dollar when they needed it. Other than that, all she did was talk on the phone.

Ezel wasn't home when Jinger got there. She put the money that had gotten drop off while she was there in the closet exactly were he had told her to put it. She was about to get undress when she remembered that she was supposed to go to Naysia's house. She looked at her watch, put her shoes back on then left.

****

Jinger pulled up behind P-Hall's Corvette. She got out feeling slightly nervous knowing what she did was wrong. P-Hall had put her on, trusted her, and she basically crossed him. That was his mindset though, in her mind she made the best decision for her. She use her own key to let herself in. As soon as she got in the sweet aroma of Ox Tails hit her.

"We thought you weren't going to make it," Naysia said. Her and P-Hall was seated at the table eating already.

"Did ya'll start talking about me yet?"

"Aint nobody talking about you," Naysia said getting up from the table. "I'll be back, I'ma go make you a plate."

P-Hall only looked at Jinger when she first came in. While they were talking he kept eating his food staring at Naysia until she left. Jinger took off her coat and glanced over at him. She could tell he was mad. After hanging her coat on the coat rack she pulled up a chair and took a seat. Things were completely silent except they could hear Naysia making noises with the dishes fixing Jinger's plate. Either of them would look at each other. Naysia came back, sat Jinger's plate in front of her, then sat back down.

"Thank you."

"Your welcome. Well now that we're all here could ya'll two get to talking."

P-Hall stuck another spoon full of food in his mouth, took the napkin off the table then started wiping his mouth. Both of the ladies were looking at him waiting to hear what he had to say.

"I don't really have anything to say," he said gesturing with his hands like he had nothing.

"I don't either," Jinger responded!

They both were there because it's what Naysia wanted, not because they wanted to be there.

"I'ma just let you know that it's an S.O.S out on ya boy, so don't get caught slipping with him. Dudes are not going to stop their mission because you with him. It don't work like that."

"Aunt Naysia is this what you told me to come here for, so I could be threatened?"

"That's not a threat, that's real."

"Well, whatever. Are you done, because I have to go?"

"Sit back down Jinger, nobody is attacking you. You need to stop with that attitude you got."

"I don't have an attitude."

"Not with me, but with P-Hall. Why did you start something and not finish?"

"I was, but he said he was done with me so…."

"That's because I know you was on some bullshit, lying. You live with dude. You supposed to tell me where he live, not start living with him."

Jinger was at a lost of words, she just sat there with her arms folded.

"So what happened," Naysia asked?"

"I don't know, I started feeling him. I fell in love with him."

"You aint in love with him. You in love with what he doing for you," P-Hall said knowing that was some bullshit.

"Well, it is what it is," Jinger responded with a snap in her neck.

"I knew you getting involved with this was a bad idea," Naysia chimed in.

"Shhhiiiit, it's the best thing that ever happened to me."

Naysia rolled her eyes at her and kept saying what she was going to say. "Whatever don't let him know anything about us. Don't bring him here or anything."

"I'm not, he don't know anything about either of ya'll. Look P-Hall, I'm not on no bullshit. I messed things up for you. I got emotionally involved, but I got some friends that mess with his boys Sony and Green Eyes. If you want I can find out where they stay."

"I'm good, I got my way of doing things."

Jinger shrugged her shoulders while looking at her Aunt. "Hey, I offered. Anyway, thanks for the meal Aunt Naysia. It was delicious. I always appreciate the things you do for me. I'll call you. P-Hall, just to let you know I don't' have any problems with you."

Jinger hugged her Aunt and left. Naysia turned around and seen that P-Hall was mad. She knew the only reason he didn't hurt Jinger already was because of her. While collecting the plates she wanted to make sure that was still the case. "I hope you didn't mean what you said about if she with him things can happen to her too."

"Come on now, you know how the streets are. I'm not going to purposely do anything to her. She better stay away from dude though."

CHAPTER 21

JINGER MET HER MOTHER AND BROTHER IN THE FRONT OF THE laundry mat. "All baby, I miss you," her mother said giving her a great big hug. Afterwards Jinger bent down and quickly kissed her brother on the cheek.

"Ill, don't be kissing on me," he said wiping his cheek.

Jinger didn't pay him any mind. She took them in the laundry mat and introduced them to some of the regulars that she had gotten to know over the weeks. Then she took them into the back office and showed them how she basically does nothing.

"I'm so proud of you," her mother said.

"Keep it real mom, you thought I was lying?"

"No, I just had to see it for myself."

While they were in the office talking Ezel walked in. They turned looking at him. Jinger hurried to introduce the man that was making her a happy woman.

"Mom, this is my man Ezel. Ezel this is my mother and brother."

"It's nice to meet you Ms. Mayfield."

Jinger sat back and watched as Ezel won her mother over. They chatted for a good ten minutes before Jinger's mom began to leave.

"When the last time you heard from your aunt," her mother asked on her way out?

"I ate dinner at her house last night."

"We're going to pay her a surprise visit right now."

Ezel remembered when he first met Jinger she said that she was at her aunt's house. He figured they were talking about the one that lived there. While they were talking it dawn on him that he had almost forgot what he initially went to his office to get. He hurried up and doubled back. When he came out Jinger was at her mom's car. His Bentley was parked right in front of it.

"Is that his car," Jinger's mom asked surprised? It was clear to her now. Just when she thought her daughter was staying out of trouble. She knew that if Ezel was a drug dealer like she thought then her daughter could be in more trouble than ever before.

****

Sony and Stacy sat at a table in Hooters eating and drinking. Nobody he knew frequented this spot, so he did.

"You sure are friendly with these waitresses," Stacy said.

"They're ma peoples, I come here often."

"You ever mess with any of them?

"Come on now, would you like if I asked you how many dicks you got under ya belt."

"I'll tell you, five."

"Alright, and I'm deaf, dumb, and blind."

Stacy started giggling knowing that it was some bullshit. "Did Ezel get his car back, she asked concerned?"

"Yeah, he been got that back."

"That night was crazy, Jinger was arguing with some guy."

"You think he the one who shot the car up?"

"Hell yeah, he was pissed."

"What he looked like?"

"Brown skin, real low cut, big beard, a little taller than me."

Sony was trying to figure out who could it be. "What was they arguing about?"

"I don't know. He was mad at her for something."

"Let me find out Jinger cheating on ma boy. She going to fuck around and get her head knocked off."

Sony sounded like he was taking it lightly, but he was dead serious. He kept thinking about the description she gave him. It was bothering him because he couldn't put his finger on it. After he dropped her off he called Ezel.

"Yo," Ezel said answering.

"Yo bro, the chick Stacy just told me that before that shit happened to ya car Jinger was arguing with some dude. Did she tell you about that?"

"Nah, but I'm going to ask her now that you said something. Was it supposed to be somebody she was messing with?"

"I don't know. Stacy didn't know him. It just don't sound right to me. That's why I'm telling you. You might want to check in to it."

"Alright, good looking."

****

Immediately after getting off the phone Ezel went upstairs to the bathroom where Jinger was at.

"Who were you arguing with the day ma car got hit up?"

"Arguing? Oh, probably dude that tried to run some weak game. It wasn't nothing, really."

"That was the best you could come up with," he asked staring at her as if she should try again.

Ezel looked at her trying to determine if she was lying or not. She tried to make it seem like it was nothing but to him it was something. It had to be if dude shot his car up. Plus, the thought of her arguing with someone sounded ridiculous. He had yet to see that side of her but he knew how some dudes could be when they got rejected.

"You think he the one who did that to ma car?"

"I don't know. I don't even know if he knew that was the car I was driving. He might have saw us in it."

"I'ma take ya word because I trust you. Don't ever lye to me though. Lying, cheating, and stealing all go hand and hand. Them type of people can't be trusted. They don't get far in life," he said before leaving.

Jinger put that in the category with the rest of his sly threats. By now she was used to him slipping things in there that would have her thinking twice about crossing him. Getting threatened had become real irritating, especially since she no longer planned on doing anything to cross him. After fixing her hair she found Ezel in the basement lifting weights. He was shirtless in some basketball shorts and a pair of red and black Jorden 11. She became instantly turned on by the sight of his pumped-up muscles glistening with sweat. Ezel turned the music down as she approached.

"What's good," he asked sitting on the bench taking deep breaths?

Jinger stood in front of him in a light blue spaghetti strap silk gown. It came down just below her butt cheeks. It was something she liked to wear around the house to be comfortably sexy.

"You know you don't have to keep telling me the same thing over and over."

"What do you mean," he asked smiling? He found her approach amusingly sexy.

"I mean you keep threatening me. You don't have to do that. I got it the first time. Don't cross you, I'm not. I love you, why would I mess up what we have. You don't have to worry about me doing anything or messing with anybody else."

Jinger meant every word. She shocked herself when she began tearing up. She stood there looking down at him with two puddles in her eyes.

"You sexy as hell," he stated! She tried to fight off a smile but couldn't help it. "Come here, you know I love you. I just be wanting to make sure you with me," he said as he stood up wrapping his arms around her.

"I am with you."

He kissed her soft lips and neck, backing her up to the wall.

"I told you how I was," he said in between kisses."

"I know but you said you trust me. I'm your woman. If you can't trust me, then who can you trust?"

Ezel didn't respond. He just kept kissing and feeling on her. There was nothing but breathing noises as they kissed one another. It had gotten to a point where he couldn't take it any longer. He lifted her gown over her head, then pulled down her blue and white Victoria Secret panties. Bout time she stepped out of them he already had his shorts down. He lifted her against the wall and started making love to her.

****

"Stop Green Eyes, I'm trying to get ready," Shay playfully said. She was really loving the attention Green Eyes was giving her. She looked at herself in the mirror while lotioning up. Green Eyes kept trying to get some sex. He couldn't help himself. Her ass was too fat, looking too good. He stood behind her with his hand on her hips poking her butt with his manz.

"Ding Dong."

"See, that's Jinger here to get me. Go get the door."

Green Eyes blew out hot air, then slapped her on the ass.

"Boy!" When she turned around he was on his way out of the room. She was left there trying to rub the sting out.

Green Eyes opened the door and seen Jinger standing there looking stunning as usual.

"Welcome to my humble abode," he said letting her in. He had a nice little house. Before staying at her aunt's or Ezel's house she might have been impressed but now she was used to luxury.

"Are you alright," Jinger asked seeing that he didn't have any shirt, shoes, or socks on and his manz was poking through his sweatpants?"

"I'm good. Just ready to go, why you want to go?"

"Go where?"

"You know, a round or two," he said grabbing on himself."

"You need to stop playing like that." She tried not to pay him any mind. She kept walking looking around the house, but he was really trying to push up. He grabbed her from the back and began grinding on her.

"Come on now Jinger, you know I been liking you from the first time I saw you. You can't tell me you don't feel the same way. I can tell by the way you look at me. Don't nobody have to know."

He tried to feel up her dress, but she turned around on him.

"Stop," she said in a demanding but low voice! Even though he was violating she didn't want to base and expose him. "I don't know what you thought, but you're mistaken. You mess with ma girl. I'll never do anything like that to her."

"So, if I aint mess with her you'll let me hit Because I'll kick her out right now in front of you."

"You foul, go get Shay. You aint shit. Don't touch me again or I'ma get loud."

"So what, if I don't give a fuck about Ezel what makes you think I give a fuck about her knowing. She really can't do nothing to me. You playing though. I know this game, I ran across quite a few chicks that didn't want to give me the pussy at first because of their dudes, but like a true champ I always score."

Green Eyes stepped off with a smile on his face as if he knew for sure that she was going to give in sooner or later. Jinger felt like it was a big mistake going there. When Shay came downstairs she was all smiles. Jinger wish she could have returned the energy, but her mood had totally changed. She just wanted to get out of there.

Green Eyes came down the stairs after Shay. The whole time he watched them talk, staring at Jinger smiling. She shot him thirty to life. Before leaving Shay gave him a hug and he grouped her butt touting Jinger.

"What's wrong with you," Shay asked once they got in the car. "It looks like you got a lot on ya mind."

Jinger eyebrows raised and she shook her head. "I'm good." She began talking to switch the subject. Still Shay could tell something was wrong. Jinger wasn't going to tell her about Green Eyes, even though she didn't think Shay would care as long as she was getting what she wanted from him. Still Jinger knew that kind of stuff could mess up a friendship, so she rather keep it to herself. Her friend was happy, that's all that mattered.

It was about two and a half hours into Jinger and Shay's shopping spree and they still weren't tired. Shopping was still their favorite pass time. The difference was that now they had money to burn. Their stealing days were over. They could buy all the fancy stuff they wanted. They entered the ladies footlocker and Jinger spotted a familiar face.

"You Naysia's niece?"

"Yeah."

"What's up girl, you don't remember me, do you?"

Fattimah was sitting next to her daughters who were both trying on some sneakers.

"How could I forget you, that night was crazy." Jinger turned to Shay and said, "remember I had told ya'll about that party that my aunt took me to?" Shay nodded her head yeah. Fattimah began laughing.

"I'll admit it, that was a little out of my league too. That was Misti work. She be off the hook. She like to treat dudes how they like to treat females. It's her way of getting back or something. I saw her go to the extremes for her own entertainment. By the way, we got something going on tomorrow. Trust me, it aint going to be anything like the other time. It's a social, Laid back type of event. A lot of ballers and ballets. You and your friends should come through."

"Sounds good, I'll get a couple of my girls and we'll swing by."

"Ok, the more the merrier. Let me get you this address," Fattimah said digging in her Chanel Purse. "I'ma give you my number too in case you get lost."

Jinger pocketed the information. Afterwards Fattimah brought her daughters the shoes they were trying on and they left.

All while shopping the ordeal with Green Eyes hadn't been on Jinger's mind. That was until Shay started bragging about all the things that he does for her. That's when that creepy feeling he gave her came back again.

CHAPTER 22

NAYSIA CAME OUT OF THE STORE ONLY TO SEE STEVE STANDING behind her car acting like he was writing a ticket.

"More tickets, what I do now?"

"Why didn't you tell me you were pregnant."

"Why should I?"

"Because it may be mines."

"Believe me it's not."

"You don't know for sure. When I seen the ultrasound the paper said you were due in March. That means you are about five months. I'm sure that we had unprotected sex in that time period."

"It's not yours Steve. We only had sex once, and it was a mistake. I told you I'm in a relationship."

Naysia opened her car door and got in. Before she could close the door Steve began rambling. "what if it's not his? What if it really is mines? Are you going to deprive me of the opportunity to be a father?"

"Bye Steve."

Shoulders hunched, face drooping, and eyebrows raised he mumbled, "I love you Naysia."

She seen the tears well up in his eyes. It was no doubt in her mind that he meant it. Still she just shook her head and shut the door. "Doom." She knew that it was a slight chance it was his. She just was hoping that them chances was so slim that it wouldn't be.

****

They were five deep as Trudy pulled up to the club. She drove Tye's white G Wagon. It was sitting on black 26-inch rims. It was the only one in the parking lot. The scene was lit. They turned heads as they got out. They were all done up with their tight dresses, make up, and heels on. A few cat calls came their way, but they paid them no mind. It only fed their egos as they already felt as though the night was theirs. As they walked through the parking lot Jinger began telling her girls who car was whose. Where they were from and how they were getting money or wasn't getting money. She was flaunting her knowledge of Philly streets. At the same time putting her girls on game.

"Just point me in the right direction. I aint leaving without bagging one of these fools. I'm trying to be driving something foreign too. I'll move over here and everything, fuck Will. I'll tell my kids that they got a new daddy. They'll understand once he starts buying them stuff. Money makes everything better," Laquanda Joked seriously.

Her friends laughed but they knew that's how she really felt. She was always asking Jinger to bring her in with somebody. Jinger would let her know that it wasn't that easy because she didn't deal with dudes out there on a personal level. All she could do was bring her around. She had to work the room herself.

Working the room is exactly what she did once they got inside. Laquanda was pretty without a doubt. It was just her two kids had caused her to gain weight, and her baby father stressing her out from behind the wall had put some extra years on her. She was brown skin, shoulder length hair, definitely the thickest out of the bunch but with a little gut. That wasn't a big deal for dudes but when it came to a choice between her or her friends she was almost always last resort. Good thing for her the other ladies had men and was letting it be known.

"All shit, is that my girl Jinger," Misti tried to yell over the music?

This crazy chick Jinger thought to herself. "Yeah girl," Jinger responded giving her a hug. Jinger's friends were a little jealous that she even had friends outside of them, but at the same time they were happy and knew that if she was Jinger's girl then she was their girl too.

"Where yall at," Misti asked?

"It looks like everything is taken. We're just going to find a wall or something."

"Yall aint posting up on no wall. Not my peoples. Come chill with me and my girls," Misti said taking Jinger by the hand and leading the way. "You know you family. It's a couple dudes over here that keep hounding us, but they don't know what they're in for messing with me."

Misti had a nefarious smirk on her face. Jinger could only imagine the type of stuff she was really into.

In Misti's section there was five ladies and three dudes. "This Naysia's niece and her friends," Misti said introducing them to her girl. "Ya'll gotta go, this is lady's night," she told the dudes. They looked at her like she was crazy but got up after she persisted. "Come on now, make room, don't nobody want yall over here anyway."

None of the dudes replied, they just left. They must have been the lames in attendance. They all knew that a real one would never take that type of disrespect.

"You Naysia's niece? That's my girl, what's up with her," Noodles asked?

"She doing good, all knocked up and stuff."

"She pregnant and aint let nobody know? That's just like her, always on some secret squirrel stuff."

Jinger and Misti's friends were getting acquainted with one another. Misti had left and came back with four bottles of Cîroc and they were doing them. All the beautiful women sitting together would intimidate the average guy, but it happened to be a lot of money getters in there who was feeling themselves. Back to back they were coming over trying their hand. Depending on who they cracked on was the determining factor if they were successful or not. The only one out of Jinger's crew who was giving up play this night was Laquanda.

"Is that P-Hall and Baby-K," Noodles said loud and drunk.

"Dag girl, if you say it any louder they're going to hear you," another one of Misti's friends said.

Jinger tensed up when she heard P-Hall's name. She didn't want to see him at all. Her friends didn't know them, or which one was which, but she knew they would remember her having that argument with P-Hall when they saw him.

They stood about ten feet away. The ladies had a side view of them. The chicks from Philly who knew who they were stared in admiration. The Camden chicks were more so trying to find out who they were.

I hope he don't see me Jinger sat there thinking to herself. She kept sipping from her glass hoping that when she tilted it up that it would obstruct his view in case he looked their way.

"Naysia pregnant by P-Hall right," Noodles asked Jinger?

"Of course, that's why he left his girl," Misti chimed in.

Now Shay, Trudy, and Stacy knew how Jinger knew dude who she was arguing with. They looked over at her and could tell that she was uncomfortable.

"Who is these dudes supposed to be," Laquanda asked? They shutting shit down like they got star status. Should I be trying to get to know them? Shit, because I'll make ma way right over there."

"They're rich, that's who they are. Now act normal, they're coming this way," one of the Philly chicks said.

Them trying to act normal only made them look awkward, and Laquanda knew it so she got up. "Excuse me, I gotta go to the lady's room." Laquanda strutted by P-Hall and Baby-k giving them her best seductive look, but it didn't work. They were used to all the thirsty moves females did when they were trying to get hit. They might didn't take the bait but a couple of their goons that was trailing them did.

P-Hall spotted Jinger and gave her a little head nod. She nonchalantly lifted her glass a little tacitly acknowledging him back. He went and sat at a table they had reserved. The two dudes that was with them stood on both sides like they were protecting some very important people.

"That's Naysia's niece over there with the red hair."

The whole time P-Hall been telling Baby-K about Jinger he never knew who she was.

"She a cute little thing. I could see him trying to wife her," Baby-K said.

"Fuck that bitch, she crossed me."

"You was supposed to account for that possibility before you put that plan in motion. You have to think things all the way through. You brought her around money. He got money. She let you get rid of him you cut off her lifeline. These chicks think about self-preservation. That's why they always be having one up on these nut ass dudes."

"She got that. If everything would have played out how I wanted it to without Naysia knowing anything I would have bodied her for being disloyal."

While talking a waitress brung a bottle of Ace of Spades on ice. Baby-K tipped her a hundred and continued his conversation.

"How did Jinger find out?"

"I thought I told you," P-Hall said looking at him.

"Nah."

"Man, she thought I was fucking O'girl. She put the burner to me and everything."

"Yeah," Baby-K said laughing. "You aint smack her?"

"Nah man, that's ma baby. I can't do anything like that to her. She was all crying and shit. It messed me up seeing her like that."

"Bro, Naysia got you around her finger."

"You crazy as hell," P-Hall denied."

"Nah, I'm messing with you. But all you have to do is have somebody follow her. I could tell he dropping that bag on her. Look at her. I know Ezel, he not just going to lace any chick. He feeling this one. She'll lead us right to him."

****

Jinger and Misti's squad left before everything ended. Dudes were on them until they got in their cars.

"Them some fly ass chicks," Shay stated.

"I know right. We have to get up with them more often," Jinger said.

Misti's friends were three cars deep, all luxury cars. All the Camden chicks besides Jinger was admiring how these chicks was moving.

They were trying to get where they were at. The only reason that didn't impress Jinger was because she was used to that level now.

"They're doing their thing, best believe they're working their dudes," Shay stated.

"Uhmm Hum," Stacy agreed.

"Best believe I'ma be coming through in that big boys soon," Shay said bouncing up and down in the back seat like a little kid. She was acting like she was steering a steering wheel with her hands. She was referring to one of Green Eyes big boy toys.

Misti pulled up alongside of them and Trudy rolled her window down. "That thing right there about something. I see you," Misti complimented before pulling off.

Trudy had a big smile on her face. She liked that that Misti gave props where props were due. Camden chicks wasn't used to chicks being as friendly as they were. The confidence Misti crew had in themselves was evident. Jinger assumed that all the love she was receiving was because of her aunt being out there all them years hanging out with Misti and her friends. What she didn't know was that it was much more than that.

The rest of the night Laquanda went on about the dudes she bagged. How this one had these shoes on and this one had that chain on etc…. She was trying her hardest to run into a sponsor. At one time her friends would have been on it like that right along with her, but now they found it amusing because they already had what she was looking for. All except Jinger, she kind of felt like it was cramping her style.

"You can't be desperate Laquanda. We playing a role out here. You have to make these dudes think that your different. They're used to these thirsty chicks," Jinger said.

"That's easy to say when you got a dude that's taking care of you. I'm a single mom with two kids. I'm out this bitch struggling."

Jinger shook her head. She knew Laquanda was too drunk to try to talk any real sense into her. She gave up without saying another word.

Trudy dropped Jinger off at her car. A Blue S 550 that Ezel had started letting her drive after the Bentley had got shot up. When she got home Ezel was sleep. She came out of her clothes piece by piece until she was just standing there in a black thong, ass sitting extra fat and round.

"You smell like liquor, you drunk?"

"Come on, wake up," she whispered nibbling on Ezel's earlobe.

She was trying her hardest to get him up, but he wouldn't wake up. Her pussy was soaking wet. She wanted him bad.

"I'm tired yo, tomorrow," he said whining and turning over to the other side on her.

Jinger wasn't trying to hear none of that. She kept biting on his face and neck until he had put his head under the covers. She began trying to get under the covers with him.

"Come on boy, stop playing, turn on ya back."

He acted like he didn't hear her. She found an opening in the covers and squeezed through it. She turned him on his back, pulled his boxers down, tossing them on the floor, then started sucking him off. He tried to keep playing sleep but it didn't last long because he soon found himself moaning. Her head game was too good for him not to react. Jinger began slobbing and deep throating all crazy like some type of porn star. He was squirming and cringing, his eyes still closed. After Jinger got him real wet and hard how she wanted she slid her thong off and proceeded to put the pussy on him.

"You aint sleep mothafucka, I know you feel this good pussy. You can't sleep through this. You love it too much. It's too wet, it's too wet, it's too wet," she kept repeating."

She was riding him hard, rocking the bed and talking dirty to him. Still he laid there with his eyes closed trying to hold back facial expressing. She began going faster and harder until she began coming. The dirty talking stopped, she tightened up on him and her body began convulsing, then came the moans as she let it all out. Afterwards she clasped on him pressing her face against his. Laying little kisses on his face, her ass still moving in circular motions, then suddenly stopping. She rolled off of him and laid on her stomach exhausted.

Ezel finally opened his eyes looking over at her. "Excuse you, Aint you forgetting something, he asked with a smirk on his face?"

"Oh now you woke," Jinger said not even looking in his direction. "You was just faking sleep a minute ago."

"Come on, finish me off right quick."

"Nope, I got mine. Like they say real dudes let bitches come first." Then she started fake snoring like she was sleep now.

Ezel snatched the covers off of her.

"That don't bother me she stated. This is how you be doing me when I don't get a chance to orgasm."

Jinger laid on her stomach naked, no covers, eyes closed, trying to go to sleep at the same time talking trash like her ass wasn't sitting there exposed, pussy still wet. She felt him penetrate her from the back just like she knew he would. She knew that he wouldn't be able to resist all that ass sitting there like that. She assisted him by opening her legs. He began going in. After about five minutes of digging he busted off and just laid in her. Her ass feeling like a soft cushing for his pelvis. As his face laid near hers she began smiling.

"What's so funny?"

"You breathing all hard."

"Because of you, you just couldn't let me sleep."

"Nooo," Jinger said as he pulled out. "You should have went to sleep like that."

"You good, I can't sleep in it every night."

Ezel laid there trying to go to sleep. Jinger laid there looking at him. The thought of Green Eyes popped into her mind. She didn't know if she should tell him or not. She didn't want to cause problems but it was bothering her. She also didn't want Green Eyes to think he could keep trying her. She knew if she didn't say anything that he would definitely try her again. She decided that a good woman should tell her man if his supposed to be friend tried to push up on her.

"I have something to tell you."

"Tell me tomorrow," he said rolling over.

"It can't wait." Ezel didn't pay her any mind so she blurted it out. Green eyes was trying to touch on me when I went to pick Shay up from his house."

"What?" He said getting loud turning around and sitting up. He was wide awake and wanted to know exactly what happened.

Jinger explained everything to him. From Green Eyes opening the door with a hard on, to him feeling on her butt. She knew she was adding fuel to the fire but didn't hold back any details. The thing that made it worse was that Ezel knew exactly how Green Eyes was. He was known for smashing dude's chicks, but he never would have thought he'll get so big headed that he'll try to disrespect him. Ezel thought that he knew better. He thought everybody knew better.

Jinger wasn't just some chick like the rest of them he was running through. She was his lady. He was invested emotionally. He loved her more than he ever loved any other female that he ever dealt with who wasn't in his family.

Ezel asked her questions trying to see if she was lying or was she the one out of pocket somehow. He knew these types of situations well, and he wasn't the type to be tripping over a female. If he was going to do anything it was because he couldn't afford to have any disrespect on his name.

The Jinger he had gotten to know was sweet and innocent. Her story fell right in line with the Green Eyes he knew. They talked for a bit longer and Jinger fell asleep. Ezel on the other hand was now wide awake. Everything fresh on his mind, eating him up. He got out of bed and made a few calls then left.

CHAPTER 23

GREEN EYES GAVE THE GOON WHO OPENED THE DOOR A slight head nod. It was about a quarter to five in the AM. Not the usual time Ezel made his moves, but then again it really wasn't a set time. Whenever Green Eyes had gotten the call he would come take 2 kilos off of Ezel's hands and pay him later. Sometimes Ezel would drop some more on him before he paid up. He figured this was one of them times.

Ezel liked to switch up spots in case them boys were on his heels. It also kept dudes from getting any bright ideas. It was too much money involved to be really trusting people. He felt it best to keep everybody off guard. The work was always already allocated to certain people. So as soon as it came in it was getting shipped right back out, but this meeting wasn't about drugs like Green Eyes thought.

Green Eyes walked in the dining room and seen Ezel leaning back in his seat with one arm on the table with a gun in his hand. The seriousness of his facial expression told Green Eyes that something horrible was wrong. His mind began racing through the possibilities. His money was always right and on time so what could this possible be about? *Jinger, Fuck!* He thought. His eyes shut for a second and he wanted to shake his head in despaired but he didn't. His nerves caused him to look back at the door. Two goons were standing there big and ugly as ever. Their hands folded in front of them at ease. Green Eyes was reeking of fear. He was just hoping that no one else in the room could smell it.

"Sit down," Ezel gestured with his gun.

Green Eyes sat down wearing the most pitiful face Ezel had ever seen. A dead giveaway that he knew what he did. In all reality he was trying to solicit mercy how kids do, but Ezel was stone cold.

"Question; of all the females you got, had, or could have, why would you violate mine?"

"Nah brah, I would never do anything like that. You know me better than that."

"Yeah about that. That's kind of the problem, I know you. You run around here like a horn dog trying to hump on everything."

"Not yours though, you big homie. I got too much respect for you."

"That's what I thought too but obviously you don't or you wouldn't have violated."

"Nah man, I don't know what Jinger told you but you know how these hoes are, they'll say and do anything."

"That's the difference between us, you deal with hoes I deal with official women. I know my chick wouldn't lie. What does she have to gain by lying on you?"

Green Eyes was at a lost of words. He began panicking. Not knowing what to say. He seen he couldn't talk his way out of it by throwing dirt on Jinger. Ezel wouldn't allow him. Beads of sweat appeared on his forehead. He grabbed at his color trying to get some air at the same time clearing his throat so he could cop a plea correctly. Before he could get anything out Ezel began speaking.

"This is how this is going to go. You're going to tell me the truth, then apologize for violating, then give me a good reason why I shouldn't kill you."

"But Ezel I aint…. He stopped when he seen that that wasn't the answer Ezel wanted. Seeing that there was no convincing him otherwise he submitted. His voice changed from that of a frighten little girl back to one of a man. Showing that his remorse was just an act so he can live. "Alright man, I fucked up. I apologize. You should let me live because real dudes aint ever supposed to let a chick come between them and their money. We make a lot of money together. M.O.B man, money over bitches. We gotta stick to the script. That's why the game fucked up now. Dudes aint sticking to the principles."

Ezel smirked while listening. He couldn't believe that this was the best he could come up with. Nothing he said was sincere. The apology or the way he said it. He threw the real dude thing in there hoping that would resonate with Ezel and he would agree to not kill him over a female. That reverse psychology stuff only worked on dummies though.

Ezel was offended but didn't show it. One of the worse things one can do is try to play on the intelligence of someone in power. He got up smirking like everything was sweat. Tucked his gun in his waist and covered it with his shirt giving the impression that all was good. He seen hope in them Green Eyes. He immediately killed it though.

"That was a half ass apology, but I agree with you in two aspects. Real ones don't let females come between their money. We do get a lot of money together. Let me ask you this though. Because I like to deal with the principles of things too. At the end of the day that's what it all comes down to," he said standing there mocking him. "what if ya so called manz tried to fuck ya lady, had his dick pressed against her while feeling on her? Why didn't he think about them principles or money over bitches before he did that shit?"

Green Eyes began trying to cop another plea but he never answered the question.

"Yeah I know," Ezel said walking off.

Ezel's goon grabbed Green Eyes in the yoke, chocking him out. He was kicking and trying to get out of it for a minute then it was over. Afterwards they put him in the back seat of the car, took him to a remote location, dumped six shots in his face from a 38. Special and left him there.

****

Jinger woke up on her stomach, face stuck to the pillow. It was almost ten O'clock. She got out of bed naked. On her way to the bathroom she saw a note on the dresser. She picked it up and began reading

Ezel's handwriting telling her to meet him at The Ramada Hotel at two O'clock. For her to give the desk clerk her name and she'll receive a room key, that he had something for her.

Just thinking about what that something could be made Jinger smile. Everything he gave her was material. Automatically diamonds popped into her head. She knew the hotel he was talking about well. It's the one they use to frequent when they first started dealing with one another. She began having flashbacks, good memories.

****

"We've been expecting you," the desk clerk said giving Jinger a room key.

When Jinger opened the door she heard Usher softly playing in the background. Ezel knew that he was her favorite singer. The sound of his voice got her juices flowing. She walked through the dim lit room like a shy girl. It smelt like coconut incents. She loved when Ezel did the romantic things. When he took his time and showed her that he paid attention by remembering the things she like. It was these little things that let her know that she made the right decision by being loyal to him.

Ezel sat in the hot tub with bubbles all around him. His arms stretched along the ledge with a bottle of Rose in his left hand. Clearly he been drinking from the bottle. The beautiful woman he'd been waiting for entered. He squinted his glassy eyes and licked his lips. Four candles stood on the table behind him lighting the room. Jinger held back a smile as she swayed her hips his way. Her hair was pulled back in a long ponytail. She had on a pair of black red bottoms, a polo T, and some tight jeans that bent with her every curve of her body. She knew he was drunk. It always turned her on to see him in such a state. That's when he was his loosest.

Not one to waste any time she came out of her shoes, then shirt and bra revealing a pair of perky C cups. They sat up as she unbuttoned her Jeans. She always had trouble coming out of her jeans. The same troubles for her was alluring for Ezel because when that nice round ass popped out of them Jeans it was a sight that would make the cover of any ass model magazine.

Jinger was playing her part in the show by coming out of her clothes extra slow and seductively. There were no words spoken, just salacious tension. She eased one foot in the hot tub, then the other. Still looking him in the eyes. He wanted her bad. She knew it and loved it. The bottle of Rose he had was almost empty. Jinger stood there in front of him looking down on him. Pussy in his face, he was breathing on it. She ran her hand through his hair holding his head back so he could look at her. His hands crawled up her legs. He kissed her freshly shaved pussy then licked it. She moaned, then put her right leg on the ledge. He gripped her ass and started sucking her pussy. She held the back of his head while gridding on his face. He licked and sucked while finger fucking her with two fingers. At the same time rubbing his thumb around her butt hole.

"That's it right there babe, keep doing that," Jinger said enjoying the stimulation from three different points. "O my god," she managed to say between shaking as she orgasmed. Her legs buckled but Ezel kept his hand between her legs still rubbing her click as she sat in the water.

He stood up with a wet face and a hard dick. "What you doing? We just getting started. I got some make up work to put in. Let me get that thing from the back. I owe you from last night."

That orgasm had Jinger drained but she was still honey. She bent over the ledge and tutted that thing up. Her hands folded in front of her as she waited for him. Before he penetrated her he wiped the suds off of her butt. He began dogging her from the back just how she liked it. He went hard for about five minutes straight but couldn't bust. He didn't know if it was because he was tired, drunk, or if it was the hot tub, but his man was a little limp.

Jinger was still moaning with every thrust until he pulled out. That's when she turned around asked him, "what was wrong?"

"Nothing, let's get out of here."

He stepped out of the hot tub first taking her hand to help her out. They began kissing pressing their bodies against one another. That's when he felt his manz rock back up again. Jinger grabbed it and squeezed it. That turned him on even more. She bit his face and he moaned in pleasure. He backed her up to the little table. She let go of his dick sat on the table and threw her legs up making it easy for him. He put them legs on his shoulders and started going in.

At first he was just in it regular then he took her right leg off his shoulder and began biting, sucking, and French kissing her calf while still stroking. His eyes were closed. She was looking at him loving it. Her pussy was soaked. She loved that there wasn't any part of her body that he wouldn't put his mouth on. He gave every inch of her body the attention it needed.

As he was about to come he put her leg back on his shoulder and started going extra H.A.M. She yelled in ecstasy. Calling his name as he drilled away. When he bust off he let out his own noise. It was more like grunts, or a suppressed roar. A victory call that relieved him of his world of troubles. He felt like he had just conquered. He was in deep, cheeks clinched, holding on to her tight. It took him a couple of minutes to pull out. When he did, he went to the bed and laid down.

"Hand me the remote," he commanded like a born king. He laid there with both hands behind his head watching her as she brung it to him. She laid right by his side. Her right leg resting on his thigh right near his manz.

"You said you had something for me," She said rubbing his chest.

"I said that to get you here," he said smirking.

"For real, why you be playing like that?"

"I know what moves you. I did want to tell you that you don't ever have to worry about Green Eyes again. You aint even going to see him again."

The look in his eyes said that he did more than just scared him away. She wanted to know more but knew better than to ask. She was bothered by the thought that he might have killed him. Another man died because of her. That messed with her conscious. She laid there regretting saying anything. "You know you the first woman I ever gave my heart to." Now Ezel laid on his side leaning his head on his hand looking at her. "I don't think it's anything that I wouldn't do for you. For real, I really love you. I never thought I'll tell a female that and actually mean it."

Jinger cracked a smile. Flattered she blushed. Them words made her forget her regrets that fast. "Why not," she asked?

"I don't know, it's just how I am. I don't trust dudes in the game and I definitely don't trust these wretched chicks. Secretly I always wanted to give my heart to a woman. The right woman though. You came a long and I feel as though you're the right woman."

"Why me?"

"I could ask you the same thing. Just because I pushed up don't mean you had to like me. I feel like you different from the rest. You weren't impressed by me or my cars how other chicks be. You weren't materialistic. Even though now I think I created a monster, but for the most part you were you. I feel like I'm able to get to know you for you. It's hard to meet genuine people."

On hearing that Jinger turned her eyes from him and stared at the ceiling. Her hands folded on her stomach. Her conscious bothered her again. The fact that she wasn't a genuine person, that their relationship didn't began as something sincere. She felt bad because she fell in love with him. Even though he loved her, he didn't love her for her like he thought. He loved the woman she was pretending to be. The woman P-Hall had told her to become. *It's wrong, but it's too late. What about my feelings, she thought?* She was too in love, plus she loved the life that he provided. *I'm in too deep to turn back now, fuck that,* she thought checking herself. *It is what it is.*

Ezel kept talking but she didn't hear him until he kissed her taking her out of her zone.

"Did you hear me?"

"Of course."

"That's all I need to know."

"He leaned in and they began kissing. He fondled her until they both became aroused again, then he turned her on her side and started hitting it.

****

Sony was strapped every time he went to Camden. This evening wasn't any different. His Audi s8 sat up real bossy on its 24 inches as he floated through the city turning heads. The clouds blocked the sun, it smelt like it was about to rain. He pulled over on MT. Ephraim, got out and gave his cousin Cody dap.

"What's good with you," Cody asked?"

"I'm good. This thing right here doing numbers," Sony said referring to the traps that was coming back and forth to cop drugs.

MT. Ephraim is a main strip with a bunch of stores. Right in the mist of everything was a 24-hour cocaine flow. It was getting dark and all the other stores were closing except Cody's spot.

"Imagine you had dope out here."

"This aint the spot for that. I'll leave the dope game up to you. I'ma coke boy," Cody responded to Sony's suggestion. He had been trying to bring Cody in with his squad for the longest, but Cody had his own squad. They were getting coke money. None of them dealt with dope.

"I feel you. Just know that the option is always there. I came to talk to you about some other stuff though. Come on, let's get away from here. I got this thing on ma hip," Sony said referring to his gun.

"So do about five other dudes out here including me," Cody replied.

"You bugging," Sony said because how he was standing out there. They walked to Temples Pizza Store and stood out front.

"What's on ya mind cuz?"

"This chick Stacy I'm dealing with. You know her?"

"That name don't ring a bell, Why?"

"She from out here somewhere so you know I gotta do my homework on her. I guess it's a good thing that you don't know her cause I know you and ya dudes probably ran through most of these chicks out here."

Cody thought of the name while nodding his head in agreement because what Sony said about him and his dudes smashing must of the chicks out there was definitely true.

"How she look?"

"Little cute brown skin young thing with a stuffy."

"Nah, I don't think I know her. Did she say what part of the hood she from?"

"I can't remember if she did. What about her friend Jinger?"

"Jinger? Real light skin, be wearing that bright burgundy hair? Kind of tall?"

Sony nodded his head yeah to every description his said.

"Yeah, I know who you talking about. She from Centerville. Only reason I remember her is because I pushed up on her one day and she aint give me no play. You know that's unusual. I'll never forget that. I'm used to these chicks doing whatever thinking they going to get a couple of dollars. She was acting kind of stuck up. I wanted to throw a ten-stack biscuit ninety mile an hour at her face but decided not to. Bitches like her come a dime a dozen, aint no need to sweat them. Plus, after I heard how she was on it I was glad she aint give me no play."

"How she on it," Sony asked pulling out his phone? He found a picture of Stacy and handed Cody his phone.

"This her friend," Cody said looking at the picture. They be letting ma young boys hit. I don't know them like that because they're a little younger. That chick Jinger dangerous though. She was supposed to had set her friend's brother up. Him and his manz got killed. She had got shot too. That was the word anyway, you know how people talk. Don't nobody really know what happened except those who were there. Dudes from Centerville want her head though."

Sony didn't expect to hear any of this. He went out there checking to see if Stacy was official before he started taking her serious. He was always on point and suspicious of everything. Ezel would always try to get him to chill out. Sony knew that he would want to hear this. Especially that they were into setting dudes up. Dealing with chicks like that was a no no. They were getting too much money and had too much beef.

While driving over the bridge he tried to call Ezel's phone but didn't get an answer. He figured he must be busy. All kinds of thoughts were going through Sony's mind. *What if these chicks are trying to set us up?* He thought about how innocent Jinger was playing. *Come to find out she aint even like that. They trying to play us. Stacy aint even give me the pussy yet.* These were all thoughts he was thinking while driving.

Still cool, calm, and collective, he wondered how Ezel was going to take this. It wasn't like Jinger crossed him. *Yet anyway,* he thought trying to rationalize. Whatever the outcome he knew his manz had the right to know. His mind was already made up about Stacy. Not only because of what he had heard about Jinger but also because Cody's manz had smutted her out. It was easy for him to drop Stacy, but Ezel was invested in Jinger all the way around the board. He knew Ezel really liked this girl because he let his guard down for her. That wasn't like him.

"Hello," Sony asked answering his phone while still driving. *How convenient,* he thought as he heard Stacy's voice on the other end of the phone. He was done with her but since he never hit a part of him still wanted some. He was being nonchalant about their conversation. She could tell by the tone of his voice something was wrong so she asked him.

"Nothing, I'm good. It's crazy you called because I was just think-ing about you. Ma dick hard as hell right now."

"From you thinking about me?"

"Yeah, I'm trying to see you right now. We can get a room somewhere."

"I don't know if I'm ready for that yet."

Sony wasn't beat for the bullshit. "Well look, call me when you are. Only little girls don't know when they're ready. I'm a grown man, I can't play games with you."

Sony ended their conversation, he meant what he said. Whatever she was trying to do wasn't going to work on him. He was too smart. She called right back like he thought she would.

"It's like that?"

"Not really but it's been almost a month. What you think I'm supposed to wait until we get married?"

Stacy seen that her little innocent trick wasn't working anymore. She knew that she'll lose his attention if she didn't give it up soon, but she wanted to see how long it'll last. It wasn't like she had stop having sex. She just wasn't having it with him.

"What's up, I'm trying to see you."

Stacy knew what time it was. She wasn't trying to lose him.

"Are you going to come get me?"

"Where you at?"

"Home."

"I'll call you a Lyft and have them bring you to the hotel I'm at."

Nothing else was going to be on her terms. Sony wanted to make sure that he wasn't being set up.

****

Stacy got out of the Lyft in a bright red dress. Sony kept a serious face on as she walked his way. That whole time he was envisioning what's under that dress and thinking about how he was about to beat that pussy up. She walked into his arms for a hug. During the embrace he said, "Aint no relationship if I aint fucking. That's just how it goes. That's for old broken-down dudes. I'm in full swing, you'll see," he said with a devilish grin.

Stacy sucked her teeth smiling at his smart comment. "I'm a warn you now, once I give you some you're going to be chasing."

"The only thing I chase is money. If you don't got dollars falling out of ya ass, then you going to be the only one chasing."

"You stupid," she joked as if he was trying to be funny.

****

Sony sat on the bed naked waiting for Stacy to get her last leg out of her thong. Once done she sat next to him. He leaned back on his elbows, his manz pointed towards the sky. She grabbed it and began stroking slowly. Then she leaned over and began sucking him off. She was going down a little then back up. Looking down at her head he wondered how long she was going to continue to play games. She was trying to act like she didn't know what she was doing but he wasn't buying it. He palmed the back of her head while she was going down and slammed it down.

"AAhhgg," She gagged and jumped up coughing holding her neck. Eyes watery, slobbering from the mouth trying to catch her breath. "You trying to kill me," she said when she finally stopped coughing.

"You playing. I'm trying to get busy. You was talking all this shit. Let me see what I'm going to be chasing."

"I got this," she said dropping to her knees in front of him. She cuffed his balls massaging them while giving him head. She tried to turn up on him giving way more effort. It looked like she was trying to give her best, but Sony sat back shaking his head. He was used to better. Her good wasn't good enough. He was used to females doing the nastiest to be around him.

"Let me hit," He said stopping her. *I hope this pussy is better than her head game*, he thought to himself. She laid back on the bed. He got on top folding her up pinning her knees near her ears. She moaned as he entered. Them moans quickly turned into screams as he began ramming her, harder and faster. She wanted to move and run but she couldn't. The position only allowed her to grab him or the bed sheets. Her ass was bent up in the air. Sony pounded mercilessly. She was screaming like he was killing her, but she was loving every bit of it. All the yeah daddies and oh babies she was saying was letting him know that the pain he was trying to inflect was actually having the opposite effect. Plus, her pussy was extra wet. *This bitch a freak*, he thought to himself.

"Let me get this from the back."

"O my goodness, I can't feel my leg," Stacy said being slow to move. "What did you do to me?"

Sony didn't respond. He was serious, his mind was more on what he was about to finish doing to her.

She bent over doggy style on the bed. He quickly stopped her. "Nah, get on the floor," he said in a dominant voice. He was laid back but stern. With the ladies he was kind of sweet but he had turned into a whole other animal on her. Something she wasn't expecting. She didn't know who she was talking slick to. She had no idea that he was a porn connoisseur. He watched Rocco, Justin Slayer, and Mr. Marcus do plenty of chicks dirty in pornos. As a youth after watching them scenes he would apply those tactics on the girls he was smashing until he became a vet and was just slaying chicks.

When he said the floor she looked at him curiously. She wanted to ask why since they were already on the bed, but she just did what he said. He walked in front of her. "I want you to stretch the upper part of ya body out." He tapped her right arm with his feet. She didn't understand. "No hands no Elbows, keep ya ass up."

When she got in the position he wanted she was feeling extra awkward. The position looked like a dog stretching. Instead of being on all fours she was only on two, her knees. Her arms didn't have any foundation because they were stretched out.

"Don't move either," he said getting behind her. He began ripping her from the back. Her ass smacking his pelvis, his hands around her waist pushing and pulling ramming, pulling her hair all the way back. She tried to adjust herself on her elbows, but he stopped.

"Get off of ya elbows," he told her. Stacy didn't like this position. It was uncomfortable and the floor was hurting her. She didn't want to whine so she bent back over and stretched out. "And don't move either," he demanded then began beasting out again.

Sony's phone was going off, but he couldn't hear it over his grunts and her screams. Stacy was praying that he would come soon. He had control though. He pulled out and a glob of her juices came out dripping all over him and on to the floor. He stood up and said, "come on, let me show you how to suck dick." Hair freezy and eyes watery Stacy looked like she just had a long day but really it was only a long forty-five minutes. Worn out she got up slowly. Sony sat on the edge of the bed watching her, enjoying the moment but not showing it. This was more of what he wanted, not to please her. She stumbled a little before getting herself together. Even though he was on some bullshit Sony still found it sexy how she was standing there at his mercy.

"Get on ya knees," he ordered. Using his knees as a crutch for support she kneeled down in front of him one leg at a time. She couldn't believe that he was still hard after what seemed like hours. She began giving him head but Sony was in control this time. He held the back of her head smashing it down further then what she would have liked. She gagged but he didn't have any mercy. "Good girl, come on, deep throat," he encouraged while pushing her head further and faster.

With a full mouth Stacy could only breath through her nose. Snot Started coming out of her nose messing up her breathing. He still wasn't letting up. He kept smashing her head down choking her. Every time he mushed her head down she'll close her eyes gagging as snot ran down both of her nostrils onto him. He didn't care, he kept her head going in an up and down motion. Tears began coming down her face. She had never been treated like this before. Her crying only excited him. He was about to come so he went harder and faster until he busted off. She caught a little in her mouth but he pulled out and squeezed the rest on her face.

When he let her up she was woozy. Her face looked like a cum shot from a porn scene. Trying to wipe the tears from under her eyes she smeared the cum. She walked to the bathroom crying to herself. After enduring a sexual experience like that she wasn't sure if their relationship was going to work. She heard Sony come into the bathroom and got quiet. He had already heard her whimpering though. He cleaned himself off and left. After a fifteen-minute shower, when she felt like she got her dignity and pride together and was ready to face him she came out but he was gone. She became frantic and rushed outside to see if it was too late to catch him, but he was gone.

CHAPTER 24

"WHAT'S UP, YOU CALL ME THEN NOT ANSWER YA PHONE WHEN I call back," Ezel told Sony.

"I got to talk to you a-sap. It's important, where you at?"

"I just left the hotel suite. I'm in the parking garage now."

"Who you with?"

"Jinger, why?"

"I need to put you up on what I just heard. It aint for the phone though."

While Ezel and Jinger were walking to their cars two men crept from behind the wall. One coming from the front the other from the back. The one from the front let off the first shot hitting Ezel spinning him to the ground. The shot startled Jinger. She jumped back screaming with her hands up to her face. Both assailants stood over top of Ezel shooting. Jinger watched not able to do anything until they ran off.

That's when she knelt down in tears watching the man she love bloody gasping for air. "O my god O my god," she said not able to hear her own words because her ears were still ringing from the shots. Ezel was laying there squirming fighting for his life. Jinger didn't want to touch him because he was bloody and she didn't want to get any on her. His cellphone was laying next to him. She picked it up and dialed 911. When she put it to her ear she realized that whoever he was talking to was still on the phone.

"Hello, who this?"

"What happened," Sony yelled into the phone already knowing the answer to his question? Is ma bro alright?"

"Ezel just got shot call, the cops, please."

"Bitch I'm a kill you. You set ma manz up."

Click!

"No, what are you talking about?"

Realizing that she wasn't talking to anybody she quickly dialed 911. While on the phone with the dispatcher a crowd began to develop around her. A few of them were also calling the cops. Jinger didn't know what to do after hanging up. Everything was happening so fast. Sirens were sounding off in the back round getting closer and closer. The good thing was that Ezel was still alive. He didn't look like he could last much longer though.

Any other female would have probably been trying to comfort their man. Not Jinger, she was too nervous. *I gotta get out of here*, she thought to herself looking around at everyone watching her and Ezel. A part of her didn't want to leave him but her hood instincts was telling her otherwise. She felt bad seeing him like that.

The ambulance had pulled into the parking garage. *They got here fast*, she thought. They rushed over and began attending to Ezel. As they did Jinger slid through the crowd to her car then peeled off. Feeling bad was something she would get over. She just didn't want any parts of another situation where someone had gotten murdered. What Sony had said was ringing in her ear. He accused her of setting Ezel up. If she did it would be a different story, but she didn't. Not that it would be her first time doing something like that, but she doubted if he knew anything about that. Trying to figure it out was too much. All she wanted to do was get out of dodge. When she got to Ezel's house she packed all of his and her most valuable things including the money that she could get to and she bounced.

****

Jinger used her key to let herself in Naysia's house. As soon as she walked in Naysia and P-Hall looked up at her. They were on the couch lamping watching T.V. The anxiety was all over Jinger's face. P-Hall wanted to laugh when saw her but he held it in.

"What's wrong Jinger," Naysia asked getting up?

Tears began coming down Jinger's face. Naysia embraced her. While hugging her back she was looking over Naysia's shoulder at P-Hall. He could no longer hold it in. Naysia had her back to him and he really wanted Jinger to know that that was his work. As she looked at him he looked back at her and smirked then smiled real hard teasing her then turned around like he had been watching T.V. the whole time.

"I knew it," Jinger said getting out of Naysia's embrace walking towards P-Hall. "He got Ezel killed."

"I don't know what you talking about," he said nice and calm continuing to watch T.V.

Jinger began yelling at P-Hall, "You pussy, you fucked everything up."

Naysia grabbed her and took her up stairs to her room and sat her down. "first of all calm down, you can't come in here talking to him like that. I told you what it was Jinger. These are not them little boys who you are used to dealing with. That's why I didn't want you to get involved."

"They killed him right in front of me. Now Sony think I had something to do with it."

"Why would you think that," asked Naysia?

Jinger explained to Naysia what Sony said to her over the phone, how she went to Ezel house and packed her things, and how she was scared to go back.

All Naysia's doubts about her niece came to fruition. Jinger really couldn't handle the streets like she thought she could. Naysia kept trying to calm her down. She didn't like that Jinger and P-hall couldn't co-exist without confrontation. She knew if Jinger stuck around that they would eventually get into it again.

****

The next day Jinger was awoke by Naysia handing her the phone, "It's your mom."

"Baby you need to come home, you got detectives looking for you," her mom said.

"For what?"

"For what? Jinger don't play stupid, you're on the news clear as day. They want to talk to you about that guy you were dealing with shooting. You need to come back home."

Jinger felt like maybe her mom was right. Things had gotten out of control in Philly. It wasn't safe for her to be out there anymore. It's been almost a year since that incident with Wade happened in Camden. Dudes wasn't worried about her anymore, at least that's what she hoped. In any case she felt that she'll be safer in her own backyard.

****

He strong, Jinger thought to herself. The only reason she left the way she did was because she thought that Ezel was going to die. Honestly she felt that it would have been better if he did. She knew that it wouldn't be anyway that he'll forgive her. Especially if Sony was talking that set up stuff to him.

CHAPTER 25

A FTER MONTHS OF REHAB EZEL WAS FINALLY ABLE TO LEAVE the hospital on his own. A few of his family members awaited him in the lodge. He embraced them and they got out of there. Outside was a few of his dudes waiting to escort him anywhere he needed to go. The only one who came over to give him love was Sony. The others he gave head nods to. Still no Jinger. Once after realizing that Jinger wasn't going to show up he told Sony that her betrayal hurted him more than him getting shot. It saddened him to hear what Sony had told him about Jinger. He didn't really want to believe it, but her not being there for him when he needed her the most was all the proof he needed.

While in the hospital Ezel had let some of his family members go to his house to get some things. They told him Jinger had taken some things but when he seen it for himself he had gotten a feeling that could only be describe as a whole in his heart. Sony walked behind him with his hands folded behind his back. Things were not how Ezel had left them. He usually kept his jewelry on top of the dresser set up nice and neat. That way he could always see it and decide what pieces he wanted to wear with what outfit. He had an expensive watch collection that sat in two see through watch cases that looked like safes. Each one had ten watches in them. Everything was gone. He grabbed the cases and slammed them against the wall real hard. "I'ma kill that bitch with ma bare hands, watch me." He headed in the direction of his safe. It was still there closed. He put the code in and opened it. It was still filled with money. All the rest of the money he had in certain areas of the house was gone. "She must couldn't carry the safe," he told

Sony. Sony just nodded keeping quiet. Murder was on his mind so he already knew where Ezel's mind was at.

****

Sony and Ezel sat in the back of the tinted-up Lincoln. It was almost 1:00 in the morning when they pulled outside of Cortina's house. Ezel remembered both spots he picked Jinger up from when they first started dating. Since Cortina's house was supposed to be mom's it was the first place he paid a visit to.

Ezel watched from behind the tint as his goon knocked on the door with his gun behind his back.

"Who is it," Cortina asked opening the door.

"It's me," the goon said pointing the gun at her face. Cortina couldn't believe her eyes. The goon pushed the door backing her up.

"I don't have anything but a T.V. That's the most valuable thing I have. Ya'll can have it," she said sitting on the couch.

The goons didn't say anything. Cortina seen two dark figures enter her home, one walking with a cane. It was obvious that they were the leaders. She sat on the couch looking up at them. The light from the streets lamps wasn't enough to allow her to make out their faces.

"Where Jinger at," she heard the cripple ask?

"Who?"

"If you want to live don't play games. Where ya daughter at?"

"You said Jinger? That's not my daughter. I let her act like she lived here a couple of times. I was told if anybody asked to play like her mom, but I didn't know her. I was doing a favor for P-Hall."

Ezel and Sony looked at one another after hearing that name. "Mothafucka," Ezel cursed! It was coming back to him now. He remembered that he did meet Jinger's mom at the laundry mat but that was the only time. He couldn't remember her face. Knowing that P-Hall was behind this whole thing from day one had him furious. Now he knew Jinger was a fraud. Still some things weren't adding up to him. She could have gotten him killed plenty of times, why didn't she? The times he trusted her with money, way more then what she took. Why didn't she get him then? Also if she had dudes with her why would they leave the safe.

Cortina told them everything she knew about that situation. Ezel didn't know what to believe, but he was going to eliminate all possibilities. "Kill her," he said before walking out. Before Cortina could scream the goon shot her twice. The house lit up with two flashes of light. They were off to their next destination.

****

The same procedure took place at the first house Jinger was at, the one she told Ezel was her aunt's house. Ezel remembered it clearly. He rolled down the back window as the goon came back to the car.

"Nobody's answering the door. What you want me to do?"

"Kick it in, we going in there," Ezel said opening the car door.

Bout time him and Sony got in the house the goon was already in there laying the people down. It was an elder couple. They were scared to death. They laid in bed holding one another as the goon held them at gun point. They looked at Ezel and Sony enter the room.

"Where is Jinger," Ezel asked nice and calm?

"We don't' have any idea who you're talking about," the lady said. They stuck to their answer whenever Ezel questioned them, but he wasn't convinced. Knowing what he just found out he felt like everybody was in cahoots to kill him. He wasn't sparing anybody. After him and Sony stepped out of the room the goon emptied the clipped on the couple.

CHAPTER 26

"You know Naysia having a baby shower this week, you going," Jinger mom asked?

"I'm not going to be able to make it, but I'll send her a gift."

"What do you have to do that's so important that you can't make it?"

"Things mom, trust me she'll understand."

Jinger knew that her aunt would understand why she couldn't make it. If anybody knew Naysia knew what she had been through. Jinger had no plan on ever going back to Philly. She felt safe in Camden, moving around with no worries despite the situation she went through before. She haven't seen any of them dudes from Wade's block yet. So much stuff had happened in the hood since then she figured that there wasn't anybody worried about her.

****

Jinger was back with her crew. Now they had names in the hood, especially Jinger. They had all kinds of dudes who were touching paper coming at them. When Jinger was messing with Ezel coming through Camden in his luxury cars she had the hood talking. Her and her girls would go out looking fly posting pics on Facebook and Instagram. Plus, Jinger had all kinds of pics with ballers and rappers. When Jinger got on she made sure that her girls shined with her.

Jinger walked around her apartment in her panties and bra. Brah was still sleep when she came back in the room and tossed his pants on him.

"Yo," he said turning over.

"Come on, I'm about to go."

"Go ahead, I'll be here when you get back."

"It aint that type of party. Put ya stuff on and let's go."

Jinger was renting a town house in Pinehill. She would mess with Brah from time to time. She wasn't trying to be in a real relationship. She felt the need to just be free and enjoy herself. Every now and then she'll let Brah stay over but always sent him back home to his mommy since he liked living there so much. The last thing she wanted him to think was that he had a home with her.

When they left the town house they got in Jinger's brand new BMW 650 I. While backing out of her parking space Jinger was taking back by what Brah said next.

"You changed."

"Changed? Changed how?"

"How, because I don't want to let you stay at my place. I got things to do Brah. I might not even make it home tonight."

"So what, what you think I'm going to steal?"

"No, I think you should do something with yaself. Not sit around my spot eating all my stuff up. Aint nothing worse than a lazy man."

"I aint lazy."

"Well do something with yaself. Something that's going to make you money."

"I got something that's making me money, the block. As long as it's drugs to be sold I'll never go broke."

"What you making is change, that aint money."

"You crazy as hell," Brah said pulling out a wad of cash.

"Like I said pocket change," she said shaking her head all while thinking little did he know.

Brah had no ideal of the money she had or even seen while she was gone. He probably wouldn't believe her if she told him. After dealing with dudes on a certain level she didn't look at broke dudes the same. They had no drive, no passion, did a bunch of talking and no action. She had higher standards for herself now, but for whatever reason that she couldn't figure out herself no matter who she messed with she always dealt with Brah.

"That's what I'm talking about. You got a little crib and this car and you think you the shit."

Jinger sighed not wanting to get into it, because no matter what she said she knew that he wouldn't understand. They weren't on the same level mentally, especially when it came to the level they thought they should be on in life. That's why she treated him the way she did, like a young boy. He couldn't call any shots because he wasn't in a position to.

Jinger matured a lot since she first had moved to Philly. It showed in her movements. Her girls respected her. Where she was the rut before she was now the leader. Trudy was the only one who she still looked up to like a big sister.

Jinger dropped Brah off on Thurman and Newport with his boys. As she rode off she glanced through her rearview mirror and seen dudes out there checking out her car. She knew that they were probably inquiring about her. After dropping Brah off she picked Stacy up and their day begun.

"Is Laquanda and Shay coming tonight," Jinger asked Stacy?

"I don't know about Laquanda but Shay aint missing nothing. She a party bob for real."

"Where Laquanda at?"

"She with O boy from East, his name Black."

Jinger nodded her head. She had heard about dude. He was supposed to have 32 Street on smash. They pulled up to the nail salon. They sat back and enjoyed the moment while getting their manicures and pedicures done.

"This shit feels great," Stacy said.

"Aint nothing like being pampered. I'm always getting done up, but really aint nothing like a massage. Getting a good foot rub too. I used to always be having Ezel doing that. I got wet every time."

"For real?"

"Yeah, you have to try it. By the way, whatever happen with you and Sony?"

"Probably the same thing that happened with you and Ezel. Them dudes are wack. I couldn't deal with it, not even for his money. I tried but it aint nothing like a thorough one from Camden."

That night with Sony Stacy left Philly feeling violated. She had no intentions on ever seeing him again. She went home curled up in the bed and continued to cry. She was so ashamed that she never told her friends.

"You aint lying," Jinger co-signed. Little did she know that Stacy had left out the fact that she got shitted on. "Just gotta get the right ones because it's a lot of clowns out here too."

"That's everywhere," Stacy responded.

Jinger never told any of her friends why she had stop messing with Ezel or why she left Philly. They didn't know about Ezel getting shot up. She sat at the nail tech station getting her nails done. Her phone was on the little table, with her finished hand she put the phone on speaker and tapped Shay's number in.

"Hello," Shay answered.

"Girl, are you going to be ready for tonight?"

"Of course, where you at?"

"At the salon getting my nails done, me and Stacy. After we leave here we're going to get our hair done."

"We'll I'm a get dressed in a little while. I just got some money so I'm a be good. What time you think ya'll going to be done?

"Before six O'clock."

"See ya'll then."

"Alright."

After getting their nails and feet done they spent another four hours in the hair salon. Bout time they left the salon the sun was starting to set. They were feeling fancy. Their day had yet to begin. They went home cleaned up, got dress, and met back at Shay's house.

"We're surprised you made it," Jinger told Laquanda.

"I had to ditch them bad ass kids. I dropped them off at their grandmom house, let that side of the family deal with them for once." They all had on tight dresses that barely covered half of their thigh. The shorter the better was how they saw it even though they would continuously be pulling them down throughout the night. At ten thirty they piled in to Jinger's BMW. They were anxious, they expected it to be a bunch of thirsty dudes there chasing. Also a lot of competition so they knew their shit had to be tight.

"Call Trudy to make sure we don't be standing in this long line," Jinger demanded as she pulled over. Stacy who was riding shotgun immediately began dialing Trudy's number.

Jinger stepped out of her car confident leading her girls into the club. Their heels clicked and asses jingled as they walked pass the line not paying any of the people there any mind. Trudy had Tye meet the girls at the door. They all gave him a hug before walking in and he pointed them in the direction of where Trudy was.

Trudy sat at a table with her legs crossed holding a tall glass drinking out of a straw. They all hugged her before taking a seat. Trudy sent for some more bottles. Everything was free. Trudy was so used to being at her dude events that she be moving around acting like she had put it together. They got drunk, and cracked jokes on all the busted chicks with the knock off purses and cheap weaves. Jinger was laughing at Shay's last joke when suddenly she felt a tap on her shoulder. When she turned around she seen Cody.

"what's good Stranger, can I buy you a drink?"

"You have to buy all my girls drinks," Jinger replied.

"That's nothing, what are ya'll drinking?"

Jinger smiled at her girls as they looked at her curiously. All of them except Laquanda remembered that time she wouldn't give him the time of day. For some reason her attitude had changed, it was the complete opposite. Cody pulled up a seat next to Jinger and to her friends surprise she welcomed it.

"You here by yourself?"

"Not at all, ma dudes are always around. What's up with you though? I felt like a loser that night you rejected me. I aint never been the type that give up though."

"Well you know what they say, if at first you don't succeed start over and try again." Jinger was actually quoting one of her favorite songs by Aliyah. She smiled at him assuring him that he did the right thing by pushing up again. "I didn't reject you last time. I just had other things going on in my life."

"You mean a man."

"Something like that. When I'm with somebody else I don't give anybody else my attention."

"I respect that," Cody lied. He knew that she was lying as well. Just trying to say what she thought he wanted to hear. He was well aware of all the little tricks females played. Still he chose to play along.

"So can we chill sometimes?"

"I don't mind," Jinger replied.

Remembering everything her girls had told her about him. She was seeing pass his ugly mug now. He was looking like money, that's what she saw through her greedy little eyes. She had a nice amount of money of her own but that was slowly dwindling. Her spending habits outweighed what she had coming in, and if she didn't learn anything she learned why spend yours when you can spend his.

"Let's get out of here and go somewhere," Cody said feeling like he had her bagged.

"I can't leave my girls, I drove. Give me ya number and I'll hit you up."

"Come on now, you could let one off ya girls drive ya wheels."

"Don't nobody drive my baby but me."

"I hear you. You must be pushing something nice."

"Not nothing like you, just a little black 650 i."

"Them BMW's nice. Yeah, I can see you in that." Cody said smiling. His smile hid his real thoughts. *This grimy bitch don't even know that I know where she got the money from to get that. She really think she out here having it, crossing mothafuckas, getting them killed so she could come up. Now she think she got another sucka. Sorry baby not going to happen.*

****

"Hello."

"Yo cuz, remember that chick you told me to keep an eye out for?"

"You found her?"

"I'm ready to serve her to you on a plate. Ma dudes don't do this type of stuff for free, and if it aint for me I aint coming out of my pockets so how bad ya manz really want her?"

"Bad, you just don't know. It's personal. Ya'll don't have to touch a hair in her body. Give her to us and he got you. Money aint a thing."

"Say no more, when she get at me I'ma call you to put ya'll on point."

****

Ezel was knocked out sleep with a new lady by his side when he received a call from Sony.

"You aint going to believe this," Sony said excited.

"Can it wait," he asked laying there in bed with his eyes closed?

"Nah, it's about Jinger."

Ezel's eyes popped open and he sat up. He was wide awake now. "I'm listening."

"Ma cousin from Camden ran into her." He said, "he going to call me when she call him. It's going to cost though."

"I'm willing to pay whatever for that little slimy bitch. I'm going to show her how much love hurts."

"I told him you really wanted her so don't harm a hair on her little body."

"Yeah, I want her unharmed," he said thinking of the most nefarious thoughts. Ezel caught himself getting too excited. "Just give her to me," he continued in a low sinister voice.

CHAPTER 27

"*I'LL MAKE LOVE TO YOU, LIKE YOU WANT ME TO, AND I'LL HOLD you tight, baby all though the night.*"

Jinger shook her head smiling as she walked in the house and seen her mom singing Boys to Men while cleaning up. When she turned the radio down her mother's head whipped around.

"You was in the zone mom."

"I was out there baby. They don't make music like that no more. That's that baby making music, not that in the club stuff ya'll be listening to. You early."

"I know, I was already up so...."

"Did you find another job?"

"I haven't been looking."

"How are you getting money then? You know what, I don't even want to know," she said waving her cleaning rag at Jinger. "I'm going to go get myself together."

While Jinger mom was upstairs Jinger raided the refrigerator for something to eat. While snacking on the little Nature Valley bars she found she started going through the china closet looking at things that brought back memories. All the nick knacks, pictures, and track meet trophies reminded her of a time when she was safe, sheltered by her mother's love. If she would have known what the world had in store for her she wouldn't have been so anxious to grow up. She was holding her old cheer leading trophy when her mom came downstairs.

"You ready?"

"How long you took I thought you was putting on make-up."

"We're only going food shopping. Believe me we are not going to see any men in Pathmark."

****

Jinger and her mom decided to stop at I-Hop to have breakfast before they went shopping. Jinger's mom was talking and she had Jinger's undivided attention until a familiar face walk in causing Jinger to lose focus.

Her mother had noticed a change in her mood. "What's wrong," she asked? Jinger hadn't said anything but her mother was already in the process of turning around to see who this distraction was. "You know him?"

Jinger nodded her head giving the impression that she really didn't want to talk about it. The waiter brung them their breakfast and they began eating. While slicing her pancakes Jinger secretly hoped that he would sit at a table on the other side but against her wishes he started heading her way. She didn't even try to hide. She knew that it was no use. They caught eye contact and she smiled like she was really happy to see him.

"What's the chance? What's good Jinger," Qadir asked before catching himself? "Oh, excuse me, how are you doing Ms.," he said speaking to Jinger's mom.

"I'm fine," her mother responded back smiling.

"How you been Jinger?"

"I'm good."

"You don't know how long I been trying to get up with you. Can I talk to you in private right quick?"

"I'll be back mom," Jinger said getting out of her seat. Her and Qadir walked away and sat at an empty table out of ear shot of her mom.

"What was you looking for me for," Jinger asked with an attitude?

"Dam, It's like that?"

"I can't mess with you like that Qadir. You put me through hell. I had to leave the hood after that stuff. Dudes was talking about killing me, plus you shot me. You aint say nothing about shooting me. You think I would have agreed to let you shoot me? Hell no! On top of that you said that I was going to get some money out of it and I didn't."

Whenever Jinger thought about that situation she got upset. It was coming out the more she talked.

"Hold up hold up, what you mean I didn't hit you? I gave Shay ten stacks to give to you."

"You gave Shay ten thousand to give to me? She didn't give me anything."

"She aint give it to you," Qadir asked sounding disappointed?

"No, why would you give it to her anyway?"

Before when Qadir met Jinger she was laid back and quiet. Now she was very outspoken. He noticed the difference.

"I couldn't find you. Ya'll friends, that's my cousin, how else was I going to find you? I thought I was doing you some justice."

What he said sounded good and may actually had been true, but it didn't matter to her because at the end of the day she still didn't have the money.

"So all this time you were holding animosity towards me?"

Jinger nodded her head yeah.

"I'm not a bad guy Jinger, despite what you might think. I wouldn't do you like that. I like you," he said reaching across the table touching her leg.

"Go ahead Qadir, I can't mess with you like that."

"Why not?"

"You trouble."

"What! I'm trouble? Your trouble too. I think we're perfect for one another, you don't think so?"

"I'm not trouble."

"Shit if you not. I hear things. I'm not one of these dudes who is just limited to Camden. I get around, especially in Philly," he added with a devilish grin.

I can't believe this shit, he knows. I can't believe he knows. He don't know, she thought. Her mind was scrambling. She wanted to keep what had happened in Philly in Philly. "I don't know what you're talking about. I have to get back to my mother."

"Let me give you my number. You never know we might could be the next Bonnie and Clyde.

Jinger took his number even though she didn't really have any intentions on calling him. When she got back to her food it was cold. She still ate it.

****

Jinger couldn't forget the fact that Qadir knew something. The question was what did he know and how much did he know. It wasn't a question of rather she believed him about giving shay that money because she planned on getting to the bottom of that.

After helping her mother take her bags in she went home to put hers up. While putting her bags up she got a call from Trudy.

"Hello."

"What you up to," Trudy asked?

"I'm putting my groceries up. I had went shopping with my mother. You just the person I wanted to talk to before I did something stupid."

"Talk to me because you know how you get."

They both chuckled.

"For real though, I ran into Qadir and he owed me some money. He said that he gave it to Shay. The thing is Shay never said anything about it to me. I'm thinking about approaching her, but I know I might end up punching her in the face."

"For what? Is it that serious?"

"I think so."

"How much was it?"

"Ten thousand."

"What! I don't know what to say. Ten thousand is serious but I think ya'll can settle things or come to some type of conclusion without anybody getting hurt." Trudy tried to be the peacekeeper, but they both knew that if it was her somebody had stolen ten thousand from she would have been wild out.

"I don't know, I'm going out there tonight. If I don't like what's coming out of her mouth I'm going to punch her dead in it. She supposed to be my girl, you can't cross me like that and we still be fly."

Even though Trudy wanted to keep the peace she couldn't say much because ten thousand dollars wasn't something light. Deep inside she really hoped that Shay didn't steel that money.

****

Here we go Trudy thought to herself as Jinger pulled up. She had gotten to Stacy's house before Jinger. Six of their friends were out there sitting around talking enjoying the summer heat. All of them were all smiles when Jinger pulled up. That was until they saw how she got out of the car with the serious face, not her regular at all. They automatically knew that something was wrong. Jinger's hair was wrapped up, she didn't have on any earrings or make up. She wore a t-shirt, tights, and sneakers. Her car door slammed and she walked towards them, everyone except Trudy was looking curiously.

"I need to talk to you Shay."

Shay's eyebrows raised curiously. She got up wearing a red, white, and blue polo shirt and some slippers. She could feel Jinger's bad vibes, even her footsteps were aggressive. They walked a few houses down out of the ear rang of the others. Everybody looked on but nobody knew what was going on except Trudy and she wasn't saying anything.

"Whatever happened to that money Qadir gave you for me Shay?"

Shay looked confused but guilty. Instantly giving herself up. That let Jinger know that what Qadir had told her was the truth. Now she was just waiting for the lies to come out of her face.

After all this time the last thing Shay was expecting her to ask for was that money. She had forgotten about it herself. When Jinger moved to Philly Shay thought she wasn't coming back so she didn't expect her to run into Qadir. If she never ran into Qadir she would never have known about the money. That was well over a year ago but now what could she say, she been had blew that money.

"What money?"

BAM!

Jinger punched her right in the face then grabbed her hair and slung her to the ground. She got another hit in before Trudy grabbed her. Unlike everybody else Trudy was anticipating the situation so as soon as Jinger hit her she sprang into action.

"Bitch you know what I'm talking about," Jinger yelled as Trudy pulled her away.

Shay's skirt was up exposing her thong. She got up slow, her knees scrapped, and her lip busted. Jinger did her dirty so fast she was totally caught off guard. After the initial shock wore off Shay wanted sauce.

"Let that bitch go," she said stepping out of her slippers walking towards them. After it happened the others had got up to go help Shay up and see if she was ok. Once she got herself together, she started going crazy. A couple people held her back while the others stayed in between making sure they couldn't get to one another. Shay wanted to fight bad, but all she ended up doing was getting into a shouting match.

"All I did for you and you do some grimy shit like that. I would of gave you that money you broke bitch," Jinger yelled.

No one knew what the fight was over except Trudy. Now they all knew that it was over money.

"Fuck you bitch, you think you all that now. I' ma fuck you up, watch."

Shay pushed Laquanda's hands off of her while trying to get around her to fight Jinger, but no one would let them near each other.

"You think I'm all that, don't be mad at me because you broke."

"What? Tell them why Qadir really owed you that money. You think I don't know? Aint nothing stupid about me. I been put it together, go ahead, tell them, tell everybody. You calling me grimy. How you going to get your best friend's brother robbed and killed. It don't get any grimier than that. Yeah bitch, you thought I didn't know. Why else would Qadir owe you ten racks?"

Shay was yelling for everyone to hear, putting it all out there busted lip and all. Everyone was shocked, they couldn't believe what they were hearing. They had been gotten over the rumors, it was something they chose not to believe but now things are sounding to true to ignore. No one was more shocked than Laquanda. She was truly hurt, she stopped holding Shay back and looked at Jinger for a reaction. It hurt her to believe that Jinger would do something like that. She couldn't take it anymore tears started coming down her face. She stormed off covering her face embarrassed, hurt, and ashamed.

"That was ya cut, ya cut from him robbing Wade, right?"

Now Jinger was trying to get her more than ever. She kept fighting to get pass Trudy but every time she got pass her she ran into the others.

"Yeah bitch, I took ya money. It was blood money, take it in blood."

Everything she was saying was true that's why it was getting under Jinger's skin so much. It was nothing Jinger could do but keep trying to get to her. That only made her look more guilty. Her eyebrows were arched like a demon, her face was red with fury, she wanted to kill Shay to shut her up. Shay was exposing her, bringing up old skeletons that she wanted to remain buried. After a while she stop yelling obscenities realizing that the best thing would be to leave. Especially since the crowd was getting larger. More people were hearing the things Shay was saying, that was something Jinger didn't want. She got in her car and pulled off. Shay was still out there yelling at her car.

"Fuck her," Shay said walking back towards Stacy's house.

Once the action was over the crowd began dispersing. All of them talking about what they had just heard. All of Laquanda's friends went over to her. Shay sat on the step next to her putting her arm around her trying to comfort her.

"I'm sorry Laquanda, but it's true. You see she didn't deny it, she couldn't."

"You don't know that for sure," Trudy said.

"No, you don't know, I know," Shay said raising her voice and standing to her feet. Any other time she would never base with Trudy but at that moment she wasn't about to back down. "She always be playing the innocent role having people fooled but you know like I know how sneaky she really is. We all know what kind of dude Qadir is. What else would he be giving her all that money for?"

****

Still fully clothed Jinger laid across her bed staring at the ceiling. Her whole day was blew. She had wanted to get up with Cody but that wasn't going to happen now. It was too much on her mind. All she could think about was how to rectify the situation with Laquanda. It was no doubt in her mind that Shay was kicking her back in when she left. Denying that she didn't have anything to do with Wade's death was something she planned on doing to the death but that didn't matter if everybody believed that she did.

CHAPTER 28

THE NEXT DAY JINGER SHOWED UP TO LAQUANDA'S HOUSE unannounced. She wanted to talk to her by herself away from everybody else. After five minutes of knocking she gave up. She knew where Laquanda would more than likely be. She went over to Stacy's house and like she thought that's where she was but everybody else was there too. Jinger didn't want any problems, but she didn't know how Laquanda was going to act so she wore jeans and sneakers. Seeing Shay there made her glad that she did.

All conversations came to a halt once they seen her approaching. The tension was thick. Jinger had got the feeling that they had just finish talking about her. She knew them well enough to know. They didn't have to tell her for her to know that she wasn't wanted there. The realization that she had lost her friends was setting in, but she still had to plead her case.

"Laquanda can I talk to you alone?"

Laquanda was about to get up to go with her until Shay said something.

"Why we all can't hear it," Shay asked?

Jinger looked at her and rolled her eyes. She was trying to be humble. The only reason she was there was to make peace with Laquanda. Shay had already got to Laquanda and Laquanda had sat back down. The pitiful look on her face said that she believed Shay.

"I wanted to tell you face to face that I didn't have anything to do with your brother's death. I wouldn't do that to him, and I definitely wouldn't do that to you. Shay you wrong, you putting that stuff in everybody's head adding on to the rumors."

"Whatever," Shay said rolling her eyes.

Jinger turned her head and continued talking to Laquanda. "You going to believe what you want but I know I didn't have anything to do with it. I hope you believe me. I wouldn't shoot myself for nobody no matter the amount of money. That's all I want to say. Ya'll can finish talking about me behind my back."

"Whatever I got to say to you I'll say it to ya face," Jinger heard Shay say as she walked away. Jinger was secretly hoping that somebody would at least stop her or say something that would let her know that they all weren't against her but they just allowed her to leave.

The whole hood was buzzing about Jinger and Shay's fight. How Shay exposed her for the grimy person she really was. Now everyone believed that she really did have Wade killed. Everywhere she went people who knew her would look at her funny. In hair salon's females got quiet when she came in. The same people who were smiling in her face bigging her up were now talking behind her back spreading rumors.

"Fuck them all, they'll need me before I need them," Jinger said laying on the couch. She unwrapped her Hersey bar, broke off the first row then bit off a piece. She sat the bar on the coffee table, picked up her phone, and started strolling through her numbers thinking how she should get up with Cody tonight. *Then again, I can have Brah eat my pussy all night. That's all he good for anyway. Nah I don't feel like dealing with his loser ass*, she told herself as she discarded them thoughts.

****

"This baby got all these gifts and he not even born yet," Naysia said fixing up her house. Her friends over did it at the baby shower buying her things they knew the baby wasn't going to play with. That's how they did for each other though. Beings as though this was Naysia's first her friends were excited for her. "I feel like I'm ready to bust," she said holding her stomach trying to bend over to pick up a piece off wrapping.

"Sit down, I'll do that before we go upstairs," P-Hall said sitting on the couch watching a UFC fight.

"You right," Naysia said laying back on the couch putting her feet on his lap.

"Get these heavy kankles out of here."

Naysia began laughing. Her ankles had swelled significantly, and he always joked about them.

Rub them for me she playfully commanded. He began rubbing them without giving them the kind of attention he usually did. "Dag why are your hands so cold," She asked looking at him while he watched the fight?

"P-Hall, you ever think about moving away?"

"Not really, why?"

"I just wanted to know. Don't you get tired of that street stuff sometimes? People getting locked up and Killed. We about to have a baby soon, I want him to have a dad, don't you?"

A commercial came on and he looked at Naysia. She looked back at him and raised her eyebrows as if to say something.

"Why you trying to get conscious on me?"

"I'm trying to talk about some real stuff."

"You been with me for a long time, you know what it is. Why you asking all these questions now?"

"Because I care about you. Any other chick a love to sit where I sit right now watching you carry on doing whatever. Them the chicks that don't really care about you. They just with you for your money. If something happen to you they just going to move on. That's not me, I'm loyal. We got enough money that we could escape the madness. We could go somewhere and live in peace. Start a family and business, turn our money legit. You see what I'm saying?"

"I hear you."

He heard what she was saying but leaving the hood really wasn't a thought. He was somebody in his hood.

"But do you understand me?"

"Not if you talking the square life. You know that aint me."

"After I have this baby, I think we should travel somewhere. We never really been anywhere."

"I'm with that. Where you want to go?"

"Somewhere relaxing, where we can take the baby."

She was hoping that getting him out of his element would change his perspective on things.

CHAPTER 29

JINGER WALKED THROUGH HER HOUSE WITH SOME SEE through black satin Victoria Secret panties on with the matching bra holding the phone to her ear talking to Cody. Her black and red Gucci dress laid on the bed. "See you soon," she said in a sweet voice before hanging up the phone. She stood there looking down on her dress wondering if she should wear underwear or not. She planned on giving Cody some at the end of the night, but she didn't want him to think that she was too much of a freak. She ultimately decided to keep them on. If she learned anything from P-Hall, it's to play her part to get what she wanted from dudes.

She slipped her dress over her head and began checking herself out in the mirror. She was looking elegant. Since Cody had money, she expected him to take her somewhere nice and expensive and she wanted to look the part. She put on her best pieces of jewelry, red bottoms, make up, checked herself out in the mirror, made sure her hair was good then left.

"Take all of me right now, just wonna be the girl you like. Drive around the partition please. I don't need you seeing Beyoncé on her knees, spent twenty-five minutes to get all dressed up, and we aint even gonna make it to the club," Jinger drove the highway singing the tunes of Beyoncé.

She walked in the lodge looking around for Cody. This was a different spot than she was used to. It was an older crowd. Everybody was wearing shoes, slacks, and dresses. The older guys were on her from the door. As soon as she sat down an old head about forty-five came over to try his hand.

"Can I buy you a drink sweetheart," he asked pulling out his whole two weeks' pay trying impress her. Old head was about 5'11 a hundred and seventy pounds, brown skin and baldheaded. He had on some black slacks and a Rayan shirt. She smiled at how confident he was. She knew liquor could do that.

"No thank you, I'm waiting for someone."

"Let me keep you company until ya partner get here then." He flagged the waitress over and put ten bills on the counter. "Send some shots of Tequila over for me and the lady here."

Jinger was irritated but held her composure. When the shots came, he held his glass up. "To sugar baby's everywhere. Drink up baby," he said then downed the first shot. "Woooow," he burst out real loud saying like he was the old wrestler Rick Flare. Then he started making this noise with his throat as if the shot was burning his throat. "What's wrong," he asked looking at her?

"No offence but I don't want to drink without my date."

"Your lost baby." He took the second shot and downed it. "Woooow dam. Hot shit," he said bouncing his shoulders like Moesha.

Jinger took that as her que to get out of there. She wanted to get as far away from him as possible. As she got up dude began laughing. She looked at him like he was crazy.

"I'm messing with you little lady, you're here for Cody, right?"

"Yeah."

"Come on, let me show you to him. After seeing that she was hesitant he said, "Come on, I aint going to harm you."

Reluctantly she followed him through a few tables where Cody sat in the cut. He began laughing as he clapped his hands together. However, she didn't find it as funny as he did, but she still manage to put on a smile. Something that P-Hall taught her, "laugh at all their jokes even when they're corny."

"See, we was only messing with you," the old head said.

"The look on ya face was priceless. I sat here watching the whole thing. This ma uncle though, he a good dude. He just got a crazy sense of humor."

Even though Cody couldn't hear what his uncle was saying to Jinger at the bar he knew how he was. After enjoying a little laugh for his part Cody's uncle excused himself and Jinger took a seat.

"I see you got jokes."

"Aye, life too short to be serious all the time. I like to have fun."

Jinger stared into his little ugly face as his smile revealed the deep aging lines. All the while she was trying to guess his age. He looked older, but she estimated he was around mid-thirties, even though he hung around dudes younger. Jinger tried to find something attractive about him. All she could think about was his money. She was going to need a lot to drink to go through with letting him hit.

"Are you going to pour me something to drink," Jinger asked referring to the Dom P that was sitting on the table. His glass was half-full, and it was another on the table empty.

"You got hands, pour it yourself. I'm joking. You thought I was serious too. I seen ya face."

"I was just thinking typical Camden dude, no class."

"Wow, that's coming from a Centerville chick."

"What are you trying to say?"

"Nothing, Nothing at all. I just want to enjoy the night with this lovely lady sitting across from me." Cody had to drop the subject. It looked like she was about to start getting offensive, so he tried to put her at ease. "I figure we'll go back to my place and I'll cook for us. Show you my skills."

Jinger nodded her approval. She loved the thought of going to his house. That's how she was going to be able to tell if he was a real baller or not. She learned the hard way how many dudes be fronting with their cars but lived in apartments or at home with their mamas. After being around people who really had money she felt she could tell who was an imposter and who wasn't.

****

As Cody pulled over at the house on forty third street in Pennsauken Jinger became very disappointed. *He can't be serious, this basically the hood.* She thought about how her friends had overstated his worth. She figured he couldn't really be getting any type of money living right here. At the moment she secretly wished that she was back in Philly. She followed Cody through the front gate, up the steps and into the house.

"Shut the door behind you", he said. She shut the door waiting for him to cut on a light. Feeling like it was colder in the house than outside she began rubbing her arms. When he flicked the light on, she just stood there stuck.

"What the hell is this," She asked horrified?"

It wasn't anything in the house, No furniture, nothing. It was completely empty. She stared in Cody's direction wanting answers. He turned around with the ugliest most sinister grin she'd ever seen. Knowing he wasn't right sent chills up her spine. Before she could react, she was hit over the head and knocked unconscious.

****

Cody's fake uncle flung Jinger off his shoulders onto the floor like she was a rolled-up carpet. "Signed, sealed, and delivered," He said. He collected his money then left. Jinger never got to see who knocked her out. When she came to things were kind of hazy. She seen two male figures but that was it. When she tried to moved she realized that she was bound, mouth duct taped, hands and legs tied together. Her eyes adjusted to the duct tape on her wrist.

"Wake up sleeping beauty," she heard a familiar voice say.

The voice quickly registered, she frightenly looked up and seen Ezel walking towards her with a limp. He aggressively grabbed her by the hair and forced her against the wall. He was looking like a different person to Jinger. He had lost about thirty pounds and looked like he aged twenty years. His eyes were inflamed with hate. This was the same guy that was enamored with her before. She glanced pass him and realized that they were in the laundry mat. She thought about how she had wished that she was back in Philly. She really regretted it, it was the first wish that she ever made that actually came true and it couldn't have come at a worse time. Ezel squatted down in front of her so they could be eye to eye.

"How do it feel now that the shoe is on the other foot?"

Jinger tried to mumble something, but Ezel just punched her with the right cracking her jaw. She tilted over screaming in agony through the duct tape trying to curl up and hide her face so he couldn't hit her there again. "I'ma have fun with you," Ezel said. Sony stood to the side with his hands behind his back. Ezel sat Jinger back up against the wall, then ripped the tape off her mouth. She was crying like a little kid.

"Please, I didn't have anything to do with you getting shot Ezel."

"Yeah yeah yeah, you know the crazy part is that it's my fault for trusting you. Don't ever trust a bitch bro," he said looking at Sony. When Ezel turned to the side Jinger saw the eight-inch scar from when he took a bullet to the head. "They're all opportunist, money hungry bitches. Aint that right love?" He reached out to try to rub under her chin but she moved her head so he hit her with another right hook. "You stupid bitch," he snapped! "Sit the fuck back up before I really do you dirty!"

"I didn't do anything," she tried to say through her cracked jaw.

"What, you a grimy bitch, I found that out the hard way. You deal with deceit and lies. You like setting people up, huh? You a wolf in sheep clothing. I got something for you though. When I'm done with you your going to be unrecognizable. They going to have to do dental work to figure out who you are."

Jinger began pleading for her life when she saw Ezel pull out a box cuter. She thought that she was going to get cut, but he began freeing her hands and feet. "Take ya clothes off," he demanded. She complied, Ezel began getting hard watching her undress. "I was willing to give you the world you just don't know. I was slipping though," he said looking at Sony. "But I'm back. Now you understand why I use to be on it how I was?"

He turned back to Jinger as she sat on the floor taking off her last piece of clothing. "I told you my deepest darkest secrets, and you used them against me. You crossed me. That's funny cause that shit don't even sound right coming out of my mouth. You taught me a valuable lesson, never let up, and stay on ma shit. I hope that three hundred thousand was worth it."

Jinger sat there naked with her knees to her chest and her arms wrapped around them. He took her pants, dug in the pockets and pulled out her keys. "BMW, you doing it up, huh? When I met you you was a discount hoe. I made ya dreams come true, now look. You got ya mom and aunt killed. Both of them dead because of ya stupidity."

Jinger put her head down in her knees and started crying. She couldn't believe that he killed her mom and Aunt. "Before ya mom died she told me P-Hall was behind the whole thing." Now Jinger was confused, her mom didn't even know P-Hall. "The only way I might let you live is if you help me get at P-Hall and Baby-K. Here you go, call them. Tell them that you need to meet up, it's important. Don't say no bullshit either, it's either you or them, choose wisely."

Jinger didn't know Baby-K but she did know P-Hall. Since they had a falling out she didn't have any problems setting him up. Especially if it meant getting out of this situation.

"Hello."

"P-Hall, it's me Jinger."

This grimy bitch, the whole time she was really in with these mothafuckas, Ezel thought to himself. A part of him didn't want to believe it was true because he didn't want to look like a fool. This was proof and he felt humiliated. He looked over at Sony, Sony stood there emotionless.

"What you want," P-Hall asked irritated.

"I need to see you. I got something you'll definitely want to see. It's P-Hall I mean Ezel. I know where he at." Jinger had slipped up and hoped that she cleaned it up good enough but it was too late. She was thinking P-Hall while looking at Ezel and the wrong name came out. Ezel became livid, he wanted to hear how the conversation was going to play out.

"Jinger you know I'm not stupid, right? I can hear the crackling in ya voice. I been doing this a long time. You aint the first broad I used to get ma dirty work done. You just the one that happened to go rogue. Now look at you, in a situation that you can't get yaself out of. Tell Ezel I said try something original. Hopefully you can give his tender dick ass some head to let you go."

All of a sudden he get a call from her about Ezel, P-Hall wasn't beat he hadn't heard from her in months. Even when she was around they wasn't on good terms because she had switched sides.

Looking pitiful Jinger slowly took the phone from her ear. Slap! Ezel slapped Jinger then pulled her hair. "You think I'm stupid? You knew what the fuck you was doing. Now where can I find that fool. Don't lie either, told you either you or him."

She ended up telling him where her aunt lived. He made a call sending his goons while he stayed there with her.

CHAPTER 30

Ezel's goons rode by the house then circled around parking down the street. Naysia and P-Hall's cars were parked in the driveway. The block was quiet, only crickets made noise.

"You two go around back, make sure ya'll know what ya'll shooting at before ya'll shoot."

They separated in two teams of twos. They got into the house by breaking the windows. Naysia heard something causing her to wake up. P-Hall was still sleep. She started shoving him to wake him up. "P-Hall get up. I think somebody is trying to break in." She got up, went to the dresser and grabbed a little black 9mm. He sat up looking at her like she was crazy. "For real, I think I hear them downstairs. After hearing for himself a sound coming from downstairs, he jumped up rushed to the closet and grabbed a M-16. They always slept with their room door open but now Naysia only had it cracked and she was peeking out. As soon as she seen the dudes coming up the steps she closed it. Scared she put her back to the door and whispered, "their upstairs, it's four of them."

Boom! Dot Dot Dot! Gaung Gaung!

Naysia didn't know that when she had shut the door they heard it. The first shot spinned her off the door into P-Hall's arms. More shots came rapidly. P-Hall moved her from away from the door. He squatted by the side of the bed waiting for them to stop firing so he could get started.

"I'm shot," Naysia said looking up at him squeezing his arm.

"Where at," he asked?

"It's burning, my back and stomach."

Wrath came over P-Hall. The bullets had stop flying. Now he was thinking his turn. He tried to get up, but Naysia grabbed him.

"Don't go, I need to get to a hospital. I don't want to die," she said weakly.

Seeing his lady like this was crushing him. He still was hearing footsteps so he got up right quick and let off about a dozen or so rounds. He heard footsteps rumbling and tumbling down the steps. He opened the door about to go after them but then looked back at Naysia.

"Don't go please," she said laying on her back reaching out to him.

He so badly wanted to body them dudes. He knew he could have gotten at least two of them, but his love needed him. He couldn't let her die. He ran to get his cell phone and called the cops. While talking to the cops he sat on the floor holding Naysia in his arms.

"You have to hold on baby. They're on their way, keep talking to me."

"I'm scared."

"You going to be alright, I'm here. You and me forever, remember that. Even death can't tear us apart." While talking he seen their guns laying there and thought about the cops being on their way. "Let me put these guns in the closet right quick." He went to handle that and when he came back Naysia was fading out. "No no no, come on baby, open ya eyes," he said tapping her lightly on the face. Tears began rolling down his face. "Come on baby don't do this to me," when it looked like she couldn't hold on any longer P-Hall yelled at the top of his lungs, "Nooooooo!"

****

While Ezel was on the phone Jinger remembered that he kept a gun under his desk. She never fired a gun in her life but she was definitely plotting on getting it. Ezel smiled at her as he ended his call. He got up and walked to the table where he had a few torture objects laid out specifically for her. While holding the wire in his hand he heard movement. He turned around and seen her quickly crawling towards his desk. "Where the fuck you think you going," he said running over there straddling her while she was on all fours. He wrapped the wire around her neck pulling as hard as he could. "You think you could cross me and get away with it, huh? I told you if you ever cross me I was going to treat you like a dude."

When he pulled the wire to his chest she sat up on her knees trying to loosen the choke, but that didn't help much. Her eyes looked like they were about to pop out of her head and her face was turning purple. The whole time Ezel was talking crazy pulling with all his might. After her body went limp he still held her in that position. Then he just let her body drop.

CHAPTER 31

"SHE'S ALIVE, BUT THE BABY DIDN'T MAKE IT," THE DOCTOR informed P-Hall.

"When can I see her?"

"In about an hour, she's stable but give her some time to come around.

P-Hall sat down in the lodge area. Knowing that Naysia was going to be fine was a relief. He knew she was going to be disappointed about losing the baby, but he figured they could make another baby. He was glad she survived.

****

Naysia laid there with oxygen tubes in her mouth and nose and IV's in her arms. The lifeline on the machine beep every few seconds monitoring her condition.

"It pains me to see you like this. If you was my lady this would have never happened," Steve said standing by Naysia's bed side rubbing her left hand.

Steve was one the first respondence, when he seen that it was Naysia he rigorously began CPR until the ambulance came. The doctors said if it wasn't for his actions she would have died. He kept the blood circulating through out her body until they came.

"I know you're the one Naysia. I hope when you get better that you'll stop dealing with guys that would bring this kind of stuff to you. I love you and despite what you said I felt in my heart that that baby was mine.

Steve felt Naysia's hand twitch and her eyes began trying to open. Sensing a presence among them he turned around to see the shadowy figure of P-Hall standing in the door.

Acknowledgements

THANKS TO MY LOVELY MOTHER WHO ALWAYS BELIEVED IN me. You proved that love is the cure for a sick heart. To my Aunt Nicky and the rest of my family for their continuous love and support. Nuk you don't know but you inspired the change. Michael (Magic) thanks for the love. You had a positive impact on my life. Mike and Mally it's been a long time but we here now. Time to make the best of it. Parkside stand up, where I go we go. We going to bring it back how it's supposed to be. R.I.P to all my comrades. I'm going to immortalize ya'll through my works. LD and Mesha for showing me love from the beginning to the end. To all the real dudes I ran across, if you still down hold ya head. If you made it out, live it up. To everyone who showed me love through my journey I know how hard it is to see pass tomorrow let alone twenty years. Just know that every letter, phone call, visit, picture, and card was appreciated. To everyone who support me and brought the book I hope ya'll like it and continue to support me cause it's going to be a lot more coming.

In loving memory of Dorthy and Douglas Mease